Cowboy's
Secret Son

ROBIN PERINI

MILLS & BOON

First published in Great Britain 2018
by Mills & Boon, an imprint of HarperCollins*Publishers*
1 London Bridge Street, London, SE1 9GF

Large Print edition 2018

© 2018 Robin L. Perini

ISBN: 978-0-263-07876-3

MIX
Paper from
responsible sources
FSC C007454

This book is produced from independently certified
FSC™ paper to ensure responsible forest management.
For more information visit www.harpercollins.co.uk/green.

Printed and bound in Great Britain
by CPI Group (UK) Ltd, Croydon, CR0 4YY

Award-winning author **Robin Perini**'s love of heart-stopping suspense and poignant romance, coupled with her adoration of high-tech weaponry and covert ops, encouraged her secret inner commando to take on the challenge of writing romantic suspense novels. Robin loves to interact with readers. You can catch her on her website, www.robinperini.com, and on several major social-networking sites, or write to her at PO Box 50472, Albuquerque, NM 87181-0472, USA.

Also by Robin Perini

Finding Her Son
Cowboy in the Crossfire
Christmas Conspiracy
Undercover Texas
The Cradle Conspiracy
Secret Obsession
Christmas Justice
San Antonio Secret
Cowboy's Secret Son

Discover more at millsandboon.co.uk.

This book is dedicated to my family. I'm blessed to experience unconditional love every single day. You are my strength, my heart and my world. I love you all.

Prologue

Five years ago

The Texas night sky broke open with the boom of thunder and sizzle of lightning, splitting the heavens with a malicious hand. Oblivious to the violent rainstorm, Jared King stood on the end of the pier at Last Chance Lake, a large duffel at his side. Peering through the curtain of water streaming off his Stetson, he searched for any sign of his wife. Was this just another cruel twist in the kidnapper's perverse game?

Where was she? Where was Alyssa?

His phone rang, piercing the roar of the torrent. He grabbed the cell and tapped the screen. "King," he snapped.

A spine-chilling and all-too-familiar chuckle sounded through the line. "You look upset, Jared."

His chin shot up and he spun in a 360. The guy was watching.

Jared squinted into the darkness, searching for any indicator to the kidnapper's location, shunting the full-blown terror that had gripped his heart and soul in a dark place.

Why had he ever left her alone?

When she'd taken the chance of marrying him and coming to live in the middle of nowhere, he'd promised to take care of her. Always. And look what had happened.

She'd been taken by a madman.

Another quick flash illuminated the large lake and his heart picked up the pace, thudding at the clip of a galloping stampede. Was that a boat near the swimming platform at the center of the lake?

Was it them? It couldn't be the sheriff. He'd agreed to stay out of sight until Alyssa was safe. Jared refused to take chances with her safety.

Before Jared could focus, the world went dark again. He could see nothing. The entire lake had morphed into an endless black hole.

"Where is she?" he asked, desperate to keep his voice steady.

"Do you have the money?" the kidnapper countered in a guttural whisper.

Jared snapped on his flashlight and lifted the duffel, sweeping the beam along the large bag.

"Good. I bet that emptied out your bank account. Did you follow my instructions?"

His unwavering focus probed the storm. If only he could catch a glimpse of the kidnapper or Alyssa. "I told you I would." Jared ground his teeth at the taunting tone, but inside a niggle of something not quite right set off alarm bells. "Where is my wife?"

"You sound nervous. You should be." A low laugh filtered through the phone. "I told you not to lie to me. You failed. You didn't follow *all* of my instructions," the man said, his voice unidentifiable. "You contacted the law. I warned you I'd be watching."

Jared stilled. Oh God. How had the kidnapper found out? He clutched the duffel's strap with a death grip. Jared had called Carder, Texas, sheriff Kevin Redmond when Alyssa had first been kidnapped. He'd had no choice. He couldn't raise the cash the man wanted. Not after sinking everything into that new quarter horse stud last week. With no time to liquidate, he'd needed help. He and the sheriff had been careful, though. They'd never met in person.

Obviously they hadn't been careful enough. What had he done?

Jared's knuckles whitened around the phone. "Please—"

"Too late for apologies. You broke the rules. Now you pay the price."

"Wait!"

"Just remember, this is all your fault."

The line went dead.

"You hear that, Kevin?" Jared whispered into the small microphone hidden beneath his shirt, fighting against the panic squeezing his heart.

"He could be bluffing," the sheriff said, through the earpiece.

But Jared recognized the uncertainty lacing Kevin's voice.

A motor roared to life from the middle of the lake.

"That's got to be him," Jared shouted. "He's on the water."

"N-no! Please!" a woman's pleading cry sounded from somewhere in the inky darkness.

"Alyssa?" Jared shouted.

"What the hell—?" Kevin cursed.

A splash sounded. The motor kicked into gear.

"Sounds like he's heading to the far side." Jared squinted, trying to make out any movement in the night. "I can't see a damn thing. Alyssa!"

She'd called out to him. She had to be close.

"I'll head him off." Another motor rumbled. The sheriff's boat. "Keep the comm open," Kevin yelled over the engine.

Jared had no chance of beating the boat to the other side of the lake in his truck, but he had to try. He shined his high-powered flashlight across the water to catch the direction of the boat's wake. Maybe, just maybe.

The beam swept past the old wooden platform and he jerked it back. He froze. Two pale hands gripped a post, blond hair shining against the water.

Alyssa.

"I see her," he shouted.

He tugged off his boots, dove into the icy water, and sprinted toward her. He made it to the structure in record time and stopped, treading water in the twenty-five-foot-deep man-made lake. He spun around, desperately searching for her, barely acknowledging the engine from Kevin's boat closing in.

She was gone.

"Alyssa!"

Jared dove beneath the surface, but with no moonlight shining down, he couldn't even see his hands in front of him, he could only feel. Frantic, he whirled in the water, reaching out, searching for something, anything to hold on to, to bring her to safety.

Something long and thin brushed his side. He clutched at it. His fingers clasped the rough surface of bark. A branch. He shoved it away.

His lungs ached. Just a few seconds more and he'd find her. He could feel it.

The water burned his eyes. His mind grew

fuzzy. Damn it. He had no choice. He needed air. If he drowned, he couldn't save his wife.

He kicked to the surface, sucked in a large breath, and submerged beneath the water, but all he could feel was cold, dark and empty. He had no idea which direction to search.

A circle of light illuminated the darkness above him. The sheriff. Thank God.

An odd blue-green aura lightened the water around him. At least Jared could make out shapes and shadows.

A flash of white caught his attention. Nearly out of air again, he swam toward the unusual object.

His heart skipped a beat. Gauzy white material floated past him in a ghostly blur. He lunged at it but grasped nothing but fabric.

It must have come off her.

He swept his arms right and left, each movement more and more desperate. She *had* to be here. He bumped into something and clutched at it. Another branch?

No. Not rough wood, but soft skin. A hand. An arm.

He grabbed at Alyssa and tugged. She wouldn't budge. He pulled again.

Still nothing.

Panic rose in his throat. Lungs nearly bursting, he propelled himself lower, running his hands over her torso and legs until he grasped a thick braid of rope. Sliding his hands down the line, he followed the trail to a large tire.

The bastard had weighted her down.

Jared shoved his hand into his pocket and gripped his knife with numbing fingers. Holding it with a death grip, he snapped it open and sawed through the hemp.

In his head, the seconds ticked by. He couldn't see. He needed to breathe. The knife slipped and sliced across his thumb. He hardly felt the sting.

After what seemed an eternity, the last fibers of rope gave way. Alyssa didn't move.

He clutched her close. Kicking with everything he had, he catapulted toward the light above.

Jared broke the surface a few feet from the sheriff's boat. He sucked in more air. "Help her."

Kevin Redmond leaned over the edge of a small boat. "Got her." He pulled Alyssa in.

Jared crawled on board.

"Guy took off in a truck," the sheriff said. "I lost him."

Didn't matter. Jared would kill the guy later. With shaking hands, he turned his wife over. Her eyes were wide-open, sightless, the white gown draped across her gently swelled belly.

"Don't die on me, Alyssa!"

Jared leaned down and rested his cheek against her mouth, his finger on her neck, but no breath escaped, no pulse throbbed under her skin. Rain pelted them. He ignored it. He pressed his hands against her chest, rhythmically, frantically trying to revive her.

He'd heard her call out just moments ago.

"We'll get her to the hospital," Kevin shouted. "Keep at it."

The boat skidded across the surface of the lake toward the pier.

A crack echoed through the night when her ribs gave way. Wincing, Jared hesitated for a bare second but kept going.

He pressed his lips to hers and pushed one breath, two breaths into her lungs.

The boat stopped. An ambulance would never make it way out here in time.

"Get the truck started," Jared didn't even look up until he heard his beat-up Chevy purr. The headlights shined at them.

He gazed into his wife's face, ghostly white. His body went numb. This wasn't happening.

"Fight, Alyssa. Please, fight." He pressed his lips to her cold, wet mouth and puffed in once, twice, praying she'd cough up water.

She remained still, unmoving.

Jared scooped her into his arms and raced down the pier. "Don't give up." He jumped into the back of the truck and continued performing CPR, willing her to live, willing the family he'd always longed for to survive.

"Don't give up. Please, Alyssa. Don't give up on me, and I promise, I'll never give up on you."

Chapter One

Present day

If today's clear skies had reflected the turmoil twisting Courtney Jamison's heart into a quivering mass of uncertainty, the forecast should've indicated hurricane-gale winds, kiwi-sized hail and lightning slicing between skyscrapers across the city.

Instead it was a perfectly wonderful day. For most.

Courtney loved New York. The twenty-four-hour energy, the fashion, the events and especially her position as curator of her grandmother's legacy—one of the most prestigious art museums in the city.

She never would have anticipated the last eighteen months, but she'd found a joy she'd never expected. Then, one week ago her world had capsized. Whatever happened in the next hour, she had no doubt her life would never be the same.

The heavenly scent of brewed coffee laced with a touch of cinnamon wafted through the shop's air. The churn of blenders and mixers cut through the sounds of engines and horns piercing the door. She waited in this very ordinary setting for news that could destroy her world.

Maybe she'd been mistaken. After all, she hadn't been thinking clearly that night eighteen months ago. Just feeling. Maybe her memory of his face, the contour of his cheek, the quirk of his lips when he smiled…maybe the man she'd seen on the news hadn't been *him* at all.

It could happen. No need to borrow trouble when there was enough to be found in the world. The valuable advice had been one of the last bits of wisdom her mother had imparted before cancer had stolen her away from a ten-year-old who'd still needed those loving arms. Unfortunately, today was too critical *not* to worry.

Hers wasn't the only person whose life could change forever.

A bell's ring announced another patron. Courtney glanced up and her stomach flopped. The man's military haircut screamed his thirty-year Marine career. She'd hired him because he didn't frequent her family's social circles. No one would think Courtney, Edward Jamison's high-society daughter, would hire a private investigator who didn't boast a Fifth Avenue pedigree.

That fact alone made Joe Botelli precisely who she needed.

He gave her a quick nod and crossed the

room toward her. "Ms. Jamison." He placed the folder between them and slid it across the table. "I found him. You were right. He stayed at the Waldorf that night."

She closed her eyes briefly, bracing herself for the rest. "Tell me."

The PI flipped open his notebook. "The highlights?"

She nodded. She could read the rest later, in the quiet of her penthouse, where she didn't have to maintain such rigid control on her emotions.

"Jared King, thirty-two years old. Until about three years ago, desperate to keep his family's Texas ranch in the black by training rodeo horses and raising stock."

Jared. She rolled his first name around a few times, attaching it to the all-too-sensual dreams that invaded her sleep much too often. The moniker suited him. From what she'd seen on television, his apparent career was anything but expected.

"Jared King." She tested it aloud for the first time. "So he really is a *cowboy*?" Courtney sagged in her chair, her body going limp with disbelief. That's one she wouldn't have guessed until she'd seen his image a week ago. And definitely not based on the Armani suit he'd worn all too perfectly that weekend at the Waldorf Astoria. The Stetson, flannel shirt and well-worn jeans had been her one holdout of hope that she'd been wrong.

"Yes and no. He lives on a ranch that's been in his family for generations. It's on the outskirts of a small town called Carder in the southwestern part of Texas." Joe Botelli shifted in his seat. "Several years ago oil was discovered on his property. He went from scraping by to being one of the wealthiest men in Texas. The money didn't change his lifestyle much from what I can tell. He still spends most of his time working the cattle ranch and supplying stock to rodeos."

She could hardly wrap her brain around his

words. Cattle, rodeo? The closest she'd ever been to either was flipping through channels on late night television and landing on an old 1940s Roy Rogers movie.

"Is…is he married?" she asked, trying not to reveal her nerves—or her fear. After her mother had died, she'd learned never to expose her thoughts or emotions, to maintain control and dignity at all times. Hopefully the skill would keep Botelli with the discerning gaze from realizing her true vulnerability. She'd taken a huge risk asking a stranger to investigate Jared King. Right now she had to wonder what she'd opened in the proverbial Pandora's box.

"Widower."

Jared had lost his wife. Her heart quivered in sympathy—and foreboding. What if he wanted…? She couldn't let her mind go there.

The PI leaned back in his chair as if he couldn't care less about her or the devastation his information had caused. "Do you want me to continue digging?"

Courtney gripped the folder in her hand as if her future depended on its content.

In truth, it did. Every fact she digested from the dossier would make Jared King more real. More dangerous. But she couldn't fall apart here. "His address is inside?" she asked.

At the man's nod, Courtney opened her three-year-old Prada purse and slid an envelope of cash across the table. No need to create a record of this transaction. She didn't plan on seeing the private investigator again. She'd shred his card when she arrived home. "Thank you."

The PI's brow arched, but he pocketed the money and stood. "If you need anything else—"

"I won't."

At her terse response, he gave a sharp nod, rose from the table and exited the coffee shop. Courtney barely noticed him leaving. She couldn't stop staring at the folder. For so long she'd dreaded—and wished for—this day.

Her phone dinged. A text came through.

Come home. Trouble.

The oddly curt message from her house-keeper closed her throat. Courtney clasped her neck. She couldn't breathe. The barista called out her order, but Courtney ignored the announcement. She had to get home. Without a backward glance, she raced out of the cof-feehouse and flagged a taxi.

Panicked, she dialed home.

No answer.

Without a second thought she called her as-sistant to inform her she wouldn't be return-ing to the museum.

The cab swerved through traffic. Courtney took in a slow, deep breath. Perhaps she was overreacting. Since recognizing Jared, she'd been a rigid ball of nerves.

Despite logic trying to convince her everything was fine, her heart raced, slamming against her chest. She fought through the dread and clutched the door handle.

Luckily traffic was lighter than normal. The moment the taxi stopped in front of her building, she threw a hundred-dollar bill at the surprised cabby and jumped out.

"Good day, Ms. Jamison," the doorman commented, holding the heavy glass open for her.

Unlike normal, she couldn't muster a smile or chitchat. Ignoring Reggie's furrowed brow of concern, she hit the button for the elevator.

She slipped the key card into the penthouse lock, but the familiar click didn't sound. The door silently eased open.

"Marilyn?" she called. "What's wrong?"

Courtney skidded to a halt. Her sitter lay on the living room floor, eyes staring unblinking and lifeless at the ceiling. Blood pooled around her head, seeping into her gray hair.

She dropped to her knees, her finger slipping through the blood when she searched for a pulse.

Nothing.

Only a split second passed before the shock leached into Courtney's throat. "Dylan!" Courtney tore through the living area, searching frantically. Where was her son? She grabbed the fireplace poker and gripped it tight before racing into her baby's bedroom.

She froze.

The crib had been overturned, the chest of drawers upended, clothes strewn across the floor.

Courtney whirled around. Her gaze landed on the closet door. Her stomach rolled and bile rose in her throat. Was the murderer still there? Did he have her baby?

She picked her way through the chaos,

clutching her makeshift weapon with both hands. She reached out, barely able to breathe.

Terrified of what she'd see, unable to stop the horrifying images flying through her mind, she yanked open the door and flipped on the light.

Her knees gave way.

Empty.

"Dylan, where are you?"

She begged for a jabber a laugh, even a cry, but nothing. Within minutes she'd searched the rest of the apartment. Only one room left. *Her* room.

She slammed through the door and froze. In the center of the perfectly pristine bed lay her nine-month old son, pillows penning him in a makeshift crib on the bed.

He wasn't moving.

Courtney's heart stopped. She raced over to her heart and soul, terrified of what she might find. She leaned over the peaceful countenance and her body went limp.

"Dylan?" Courtney's hand shook. The fireplace iron thudded to the floor. She reached out to touch her baby boy's face.

Her son's chest rose and fell. He was alive.

Choking back a sob of relief, Courtney scooped up her son with noodle-like arms. The movement caused Dylan to screw up his face and let out a loud yell.

"What happened, baby?" She glanced around the room, but nothing else appeared to be out of place.

Her gaze landed on Dylan's stuffed lamb sitting on one pillow. A sheet of paper was pinned to the toy. She scanned the words in horror.

If we wanted to kidnap him, your son would be gone.

If we wanted to kill him, your son would be dead.

When we come back, we WILL take him. We WILL kill him.

Unless we receive $3,680,312.00.

We will call you with instructions.

If you contact the police or FBI, he will die.

If you don't get us the money within 72 hours, he will die.

Don't try to be smart. You can't hide from us.

With a shuddering breath, Courtney tried to comprehend what she was reading. The strange amount of money, the taunting threats. Nothing made sense.

She gazed into Dylan's one brown eye and one green eye, trying to smile with reassurance, all the while backing toward the door. "We have to get you out of here."

Bundling up the diaper bag, Courtney raced out of the apartment with one last sorrowful glance at Marilyn. What kind of monster would kill the sweet woman who loved Dylan so much?

She hugged her child close. "I'll keep you safe, Jelly Bean. I promise."

ALMOST TWO HOURS LATER, the car service's Mercedes pulled up in front of her father's Greenwich, Connecticut, mansion. Courtney turned her cell phone over and over in her hand. Her thumb hovered over the emergency key. For the thousandth time on the ride there, she considered calling law enforcement.

Something had stopped her once again. Maybe it was all those television programs that showed how easy it was to hack a phone call. She couldn't take the risk. Not with Jelly Bean. The kidnapper had come into her *home*. Had touched her baby boy. Had killed Marilyn.

A shiver vibrated down her arms. Part of her kept telling herself this couldn't be happening. Threats like this were the stuff of crime novels and television shows, and yet every time she reread the note and pictured poor Marilyn lying on the floor of her penthouse, she knew it was her reality.

Which was why she was about to make an unprecedented request. Courtney rubbed her eyes. She'd never gone to her father with an open hand, but she didn't know where else to turn. Her job, the penthouse, everything but her salary was part of her grandmother's trust specifically created to fund the museum. She didn't have the money to pay the murderer what he wanted.

She had to believe her father would give her what she needed. He had to. Even though he'd been furious—not to mention disappointed—when she'd found herself pregnant and had refused to name the father.

She'd been too embarrassed to tell him she didn't know the man's name.

"You getting out or what?" the driver asked from the front seat.

Courtney nodded and unbuckled the car seat. She rounded the vehicle to retrieve Dylan, and the driver met her at the door. He opened it and she grabbed the carrier, careful not to jar the baby.

"How much do I owe you—?"

The man shook his head. "It's been taken care of. I was asked to give you this when we arrived." He handed her a padded envelope. Before she could open it, he jumped into the Mercedes and screeched out of the driveway.

One look and her gut sank. She recognized the handwriting on the label. She lowered Dylan to the ground and gently tore open the envelope. She pulled out a phone with a sticky note attached.

Keep the phone with you.
Keep your silence. Especially from your father.
And don't forget, you can't hide from us. We'll always find you.

The note crinkled in her grasp. How did he know so much? The words blurred on the paper. Her knees shook; her legs quivered. She nearly sank to the ground. Her gaze whipped to the now empty driveway. Was the driver blackmailing her? She shook her head. Somehow she doubted it. He wouldn't have wanted to show his face. Besides, he'd said someone else had paid him.

The blackmailers had made their point clear, though. She'd better follow his instructions exactly. No police, no law enforcement. She couldn't imagine what the cops would think when they found Marilyn. She'd considered phoning in an anonymous tip, but she couldn't risk being arrested. Not before she was certain Dylan was safe.

"Okay, you can do this. You can do anything for Dylan." She shoved the phone into her pocket and stumbled through the front door of the mansion. The eight-thousand-square-foot home had been in the family for four generations, the money originated from more than a few deals with Andrew Carnegie.

Courtney had never ruminated on her family's money much. It had always just been there. She'd never been more thankful for the privilege than she was today.

She glanced at her son. Today the money she'd always taken for granted would save Dylan.

She refused to consider that the first payment wouldn't be enough to get rid of the blackmailer. One step at a time.

The foyer's Baccarat chandelier glittered high above her, though the butler didn't appear out of nowhere like he usually did.

"Fitz?" she called.

No response. How strange.

"Clarissa? Burbank? Anyone here?"

Her footsteps echoed on the marble floor. Where was the rest of the staff?

A horrific possibility hit her squarely in

the chest. What if the killer had come here. Oh God.

She started to run from room to room. No. This wasn't right. Bare rooms, boxes, paintings missing.

"F-father?" she called, her voice shaky. She opened the door to her mother's old sitting room. The blank space on the wall slammed into her. The Degas painting her mother had purchased just before her death was gone.

"Father!" she shouted again.

"In the library." Her father's voice filtered through the deserted hallways.

Something was wrong. He sounded strange, his words slurred. Courtney hurried through the double doors. A stack of boxes littered the floor. He huddled behind his mahogany desk, staring across the room as if in a trance. A half-empty bottle of cognac sat at his elbow, an empty old-fashioned Waterford glass directly in front of him.

Carefully, she set Dylan down on the floor

and ran to her father. "What's going on?" Was he actually leaving their family home? It didn't make sense.

He shoved his hand through his already mussed hair and cleared his throat. "I should've called you sooner." He let out a long sigh.

She studied his bleary gaze. Drinking again. Why wasn't she surprised? "Father, I don't mean to be rude, but right now I need your help. For Dylan. We need three million dollars."

He blinked up at her, confusion lacing his eyes. He reached for the century-old bottle, poured four fingers and swigged it down. "No."

She couldn't have heard him right. "You don't understand. Please. I'll move out of the penthouse. I'll find somewhere else to live. But I need that money." Panic raised her voice. He had to help. She didn't want to reveal the threat. She couldn't afford for her father to contact the FBI or the cops. He always wanted to fix everything. Had made it his mission to protect her from the time her mother had died.

"It wouldn't matter," he said. "I'm sorry. So very, very sorry."

"What are you talking about?" She gripped the lapel of his coat. "I haven't asked for anything since I started working. I make my own way—"

He pressed a finger over her lips and gazed at her with bloodshot eyes.

"I'd give you the money if I could, Courtney. You don't know how much I wish I could, but I can't." He looked away. "All the money is gone."

Chapter Two

Spring didn't bring new beginnings to Last Chance Ranch; it choked 'em dry in the West Texas sun. Jared King had learned long ago that his family's cattle spread richly deserved its name. It had for six generations.

Now, he even had to fight his north-side neighbor, Ned Criswell, for water that was rightfully theirs. A never ending feud he'd tried to escape for years.

When Jared had volunteered for the Army at eighteen, he'd been convinced he would never succumb to the ranch's bad karma. What a young fool he'd been. After being discharged he'd brought home a beautiful young wife and pretended he could find hope where only despair had dug in roots. After Alyssa's death, he'd finally given in to whatever mojo the half-million acres possessed. He wouldn't try to buck destiny again.

He tilted his Stetson against the afternoon glare and hooked his boot on the sturdy rail of the bull pen. He leveled the dead-cold stare that would have sent his ranch hands quaking and running for cover on Ned Criswell and his no-good son. The two burley men refused to back off. "You can't keep that river dammed up. Last Chance Lake is down several feet already."

Ned's face turned beet red, and he stuck out his barrel chest. "The water stays on my side of the property line until you stop those company men from traipsing across my land."

Jared head throbbed. They'd replayed this scene countless time over the years. The bad blood between the families stretched back decades, but Ned Criswell had become even more ruthless. And relentless. He might actually do it, just to get back at Jared's father, even though he'd passed away years ago.

The son, on the other hand, Chuck Criswell was all about the money. And the power.

"The water's running low for my cattle," Jared said, fighting to keep his tone reasonable for the moment. "You don't want to take this fight any further, Ned. You know I'll win."

"My father has as many friends in Austin as you do. We want what's coming to us." Chuck spit a wad of tobacco on the ground.

"Shut up," Ned said, glaring at his son.

Even with the same goal, the two men couldn't show a united front. A sure way to lose. Jared was fine with that.

A loud snort sounded from the enclosure next to them. Chuck scooted away from the fence. "That bull is a menace." He frowned. "You shouldn't have saved him."

Sometimes Jared agreed. Angel Maker had

earned his name. He'd nearly gored a half dozen of Jared's best hands. The black bull from hell pawed at the dirt, giving Jared the evil eye. He'd saved the bad-tempered beast from being put down after a deadly episode at the San Antonio Rodeo earlier this year. The bull's bloodline would solidify Jared's place as the premier stock supplier for the Professional Bull Riders rodeo circuit. His money might come from oil and gas now, but at his heart he was still a rancher, and the rodeo was in his blood.

Besides, Jared had a penchant for lost causes...at least those that didn't touch his heart.

Angel Maker butted his head against the fence. This time Ned joined his son, away from the pen. Jared bit back a smile. If the animal had wanted to do any real damage that pen wouldn't stop him. "He likes you."

The older man bit out a curse. "You gonna say something to those oil guys or not?"

"You signed a contract. They have a right to cross your land on the road."

"I changed my mind."

Yeah. He wanted more money. Jared recognized the gleam in Ned's eye. The Criswells had a weakness for gambling—and Chuck had developed a rep for being particularly unlucky. Rumor had it that between the football playoffs, Super Bowl and the latest NCAA basketball tournament, the Criswells had cleaned out their bank accounts.

"If you don't knock down that dam, Ned. I'll do it for you."

"I don't like threats. You're worse than your old man, King. And he was an SOB."

"You took advantage of him and nearly cost Dad our land," Jared said, with a bite. "But I'm not the pushover my father was. The Army taught me how to fight."

Ned's face paled, but like most cowards, he didn't face a battle, he ran.

"This isn't over." He turned to his son. "Start the truck."

Chuck ran over to the brand-new F-350 and jumped in. Ned followed and heaved himself into the front seat. "I'm keeping the dam."

Chuck gunned the accelerator, leaving a cloud of dust in their wake.

Jared rubbed his brow where the headache had erupted just beneath the surface. Ned had to know he was on thin ice diverting a waterway that flowed across more than his own property. Problem was, bureaucracy could take months to deal with it and the spring livestock needed that water.

"I say we send some equipment in and bust a hole in the dam." Jared's foreman sidled up to him. "The Criswells won't give in," Roscoe Hines said under his breath. "They're getting desperate." He glanced at their newest hand. "Tim, try to distract Angel Maker."

Jared kneaded the base of his neck in exasperation. "Ned was a bully when he screwed my dad. He hasn't changed. He won't back off even if it's in his own best interest. Using water as a leverage to change our deal is a mistake. He's doing a lot of damage and he won't win. Our contract is ironclad."

The clatter of wooden planks and the banging of metal clamored from Angel Maker's pen.

"Speaking of bad blood..." Roscoe raced to the bull's pen. "Get out of there, Tim."

The eighteen-year-old hand jumped over the fence and out of the pen. Angel Maker rammed the wood, and it creaked under the two-and-a-half-ton bull's weight.

Tim's freckled-face had gone red with exertion. He bent over and sucked wind, but his eyes gleamed with challenge.

Roscoe shook his head in incredulity and sauntered back over to Jared. "That kid's either going to be a hell of a good hand, or he's going to wind up dead."

"I'm betting the former," Jared said. "Reminds me of Derek the first time you guys drove up to the ranch after Dad hired you."

"That son of mine was some daredevil, that's for sure." Roscoe smiled, that proud grin only a father could have for his son. "He said he'd come visit soon, but every time he makes plans, work interferes."

"We need to get him out here, see if he's forgotten how to ride."

Man, they'd had fun together as kids on a ranch with no fences, no boundaries. The moment Derek had arrived on the ranch he and Jared had been inseparable. There'd been hard work and a lot of chores; they'd gotten into their share of trouble, but Jared hadn't minded. They'd faced the discipline together. From junior high rodeo through high school football, up through and including enlisting at the Army recruitment office. Strange how life had taken them in different directions. Their paths had diverged so much, he hadn't seen Derek in a couple of years.

"He likes his new job?"

"He seems to. Makes more money than I ever dreamed." Roscoe shook his head in befuddlement. "Not sure how exactly. Something to do with computers."

"He was always book smart," Jared said. He'd have to give his old friend a call. Roscoe had been looking a little under the weather lately. Jared couldn't convince his foreman to see the doc. Maybe Derek could.

The roar of an engine broke into his thoughts just as a baby blue Mustang drove up to the main house about fifty or so feet away.

"You expecting someone?" Roscoe asked, eyeing the vehicle.

"Not that I know of." Who'd drive a dang fool car like that onto his ranch?

"Maybe someone else on the hunt for all those greenbacks you got stashed in the bank."

Jared scowled at his foreman. A few five-times-removed relatives had come out of the woodwork once word of the oil went public.

Jared had tried to help until they'd made it clear they hadn't wanted a leg up, but a perpetual handout. Once he'd cut off the money, they'd disappeared once again.

The car stopped and the engine went quiet. It sat there for several moments until one long, shapely leg, then another, stepped out.

The woman ran her fingers through her hair. The sun gleamed off the blonde locks. Roscoe let out a long, slow whistle.

Jared couldn't move. He blinked once. Then again.

It couldn't be. Not her.

She stood still, in her four-inch heels and tailored dress, looking like a city girl who had been dropped into a foreign land. She tucked her short hair behind one ear and hesitated, turning in a circle, taking in the lay of his ranch.

He fought the urge to wash the dirt away and waited, his breath quickening as the lines of her back then the curves of her front came into view. It was her, all right. He didn't know her name, but what he did know made his libido perk up and his heart thud to attention for the first time in the eighteen months since he'd held her in his arms.

Unable to stop himself, Jared crossed the yard. The closer he got, the more he noticed the fidgety movement of her hands.

At least she couldn't hide her nerves. Made him feel a bit better, because *his* damn hands were shaking too.

About ten feet away from her, he paused.

She faced him and lifted her gaze to his.

His breath caught. It *was* her. She was here. On *his* land. Exactly like he'd dreamed more times than he could count.

Her cobalt blue eyes widened as if she couldn't believe it was him.

Well, ditto.

The rumblings of a tractor, the whinny of the horses, the snort of Angel Maker faded into the background. The world melted away; his heartbeat whooshed inside his head.

She blinked and glanced over her shoulder into the vehicle.

Her movement shocked him back to reality. He strode toward her, forcing himself not to hurry too fast.

"I'm surprised," he said, determined to keep his tone nonchalant.

"As am I," she said.

Her voice was a bit huskier than he remembered. He studied her face and detected tension around her mouth, redness staining her eyes.

They stared at each other, the awkward silence continuing far too long. What was he supposed to say? *I came back to the hotel room but you were gone?* Or maybe the more appropriate, *So, we slept together a year and a half ago and the earth moved. What's your name?*

At that moment, Velma marched down the

steps of the main house, wiping her hands on a dish towel. Not much gave away her age, except her silvered-auburn hair and her devil-may-care curiosity. She wasn't shy about inserting herself into almost any conversation either.

She shot him a piercing stare and tilted her head. He could see her interest building. A small curse escaped under his breath. His housekeeper was more like his grandmother than anything. She'd worked for the King family as long as Jared could remember. She knew him too well, and unfortunately, she'd developed a sixth sense whenever Jared found himself in a situation that could turn awkward at any moment.

Her gaze alternated between him and their visitor. "Quite a set of wheels, boyo. You must be drooling."

She sent him that knowing gaze she'd used when she knew he wanted something in the worst way. She had no idea. Unfortunately, Jared could feel the heat flooding his cheeks.

"And who might your friend be?" Velma asked with a satisfied grin, walking boldly over and sticking out a hand to introduce herself.

"I'm Courtney Jamison," the woman responded. A nervous smile tilted their visitor's lips.

Courtney Jamison. He let her name settle across his mind. It suited her. It screamed New York and the Waldorf Astoria where they'd met. It definitely didn't suit the Last Chance Ranch. Not by half.

A cry sounded from the car.

"You have a little one?" Velma asked, her smile lighting as bright as the West Texas sun on a clear day.

"His name is Dylan." Courtney reached into the backseat, fiddled with something in the car and pulled a baby from the vehicle.

"Almost a year?" Velma asked.

"Nine months," Courtney said softly, looking straight at Jared.

"A big boy then."

Nine months. That meant she got pregnant about eighteen months ago. New York.

It couldn't be. It was just one night. One…

As if in a trance, he closed the distance between him and Courtney. He stared into the little boy's eyes. One brown. One green. The baby had heterochromia. Just like him.

Jared held out his hand. It shook. Dylan leaned against his mother's chest and dipped his face into her neck.

"Dylan," Courtney whispered. "This is your daddy."

The words struck Jared harder than Angel Maker's most vicious charge. His mind whirled in denial even as the truth peeked at him from beneath long, baby-fine lashes. He couldn't deny that he stood face-to-face with the one thing he'd never believed he'd have.

Dylan tilted his head and a smile lit his face. He leaned forward with outstretched hands. Jared bent closer. The baby grabbed his hat and threw it to the ground, chuckling.

"Takes after you, boyo," Velma said. "That's plain to see."

A strange white noise buzzed in Jared's ears. He shook the static away. "How did you find me?" he asked, barely able to croak out the words.

He didn't want to say more. Velma and Roscoe both had big ears, and they were obviously curious. He'd be fielding a whole lot of questions before sunset hit anyway.

Jared picked up his hat and held it toward Dylan. He couldn't take his eyes off the baby. The little guy grabbed the brim and tugged.

Strong grip, his son had.

His son.

What was he supposed to do about that?

"I saw a news story about the bull you saved.

That's how I found you." Courtney nodded toward Angel Maker, who appeared to be eyeing Tim for a second soul-fearing battle. "That's him?"

"In the flesh."

He wouldn't be diverted by that animal. He had a million questions, but he'd start with one. "Why are you here, Courtney?"

Her name caressed his tongue, and he lingered on the taste for a moment.

She glanced away, not meeting his gaze. Something didn't feel right. The hair on the back of his neck stiffened to attention. She chewed on her lip and seemed to be searching for the words.

"You could've called," he said. "Or had a lawyer contact me. Instead, you traveled halfway across the country with our son with no way of predicting my reaction. Why?"

She straightened her back and lifted her chin. At this angle, he could take in every detail of her reddened eyes and tightly drawn lips. Something was definitely wrong.

"I came for your help. Someone has threatened to kill our son."

COURTNEY HAD NEVER seen anyone react so fast. The words had barely left her lips when Jared's gaze scanned the perimeter. The muscle in his jawline pulsed, and a flat, dangerous stillness settled through his body.

"Come with me," he said, gripping her arm with a firm hand.

He didn't take a second look at Dylan, didn't hesitate. He pulled her toward the sprawling ranch style house and glanced over his shoulder. "Roscoe, check in with the hands. I want to know if anyone's seen anything…off."

"But we've already doubled security because of—"

"Triple-check everything," Jared snapped.

The grizzled cowboy didn't hesitate. He gave

a curt nod and hurried into a huge barn past the pen holding the angry-looking bull.

Courtney had never experienced a more surreal moment. Jared didn't question her; he didn't look at her like she was crazy. He simply acted.

He shuffled her up the steps and across the wide wooden porch. He opened the screen door and held it while she disappeared inside. She couldn't quite accept the foreign place where she found herself. On an actual Texas ranch in the middle of nowhere after a too long drive from an airport that had taken all of ten minutes to walk from one end to the other.

Not to mention she currently stood only a short city block away from a vicious-looking bull, several stereotypical cowboys, a bevy of horses and a large barn. If it hadn't been for the beat-up pickup truck she'd parked besides, she'd have wondered what century she'd landed in.

"Velma, lock the front door, shut the curtains

and stay inside," Jared ordered the woman hurrying behind them. "I don't want either of you out in the open until I know exactly what's going on."

The housekeeper didn't pause or argue, but moved in a whirlwind to follow his instructions. Jared tugged on Courtney's arm. Normally she would have resisted the manhandling, but he'd stunned her. She hadn't even showed him the note yet.

"My luggage—"

"I'll bring it in later."

The curt words brooked no argument. At Jared's tone Dylan squirmed in her arms, whimpering a bit. She bounced him, holding him closer. "It's okay, Jelly Bean. We're going to be fine."

She could only pray she wasn't lying.

Courtney kissed his forehead and breathed in his baby powder scent. She touched her cheek to Dylan's soft hair and closed her eyes. The blackmailer had forced her to keep his cell phone. She wasn't stupid. He had to be tracking her. He had to know she'd flown to Texas. She'd believed him when he'd promised she couldn't hide.

She'd needed help and law enforcement was off the table. She'd risked everything coming here. The blackmailer had been perfectly clear. He wanted money. Since she didn't have any and neither did her father, she had no choice. Jared was her only option to protect her son.

After a glance through the shutters in the front window, he faced his housekeeper. "Velma, show Courtney into my study. I'll check the back door."

Brow furrowed, Velma crossed the stone foyer to a set of large mahogany double doors. "Come along, dearie."

Courtney followed, trying to keep her increasingly unhappy son calm. She rubbed his back in slow, circular motions. Velma snapped closed the curtains on three large windows before flipping on a series of track lights to brighten the wood paneled room.

Dylan clutched at the neck of Courtney's Louis Vuitton dress, his mouth drooling, his face reddening.

"I know what you want," she whispered, gently pushing his light brown hair off his forehead. She settled into a large leather sofa and zipped open the diaper bag, pulling out a teething biscuit.

Dylan grabbed the treat in both hands and stuffed it into his mouth, gnawing with gusto. He sagged against her, content for the moment.

"You know your boy well," Velma remarked with approval.

"He's my son."

"And mine." Jared stood, outlined by the dark wood door frame, a rifle crooked over his bent arm. "The house is secure. I've instructed four hands to keep watch. Velma, I could use some of that coffee cake you made yesterday."

"Go easy, boyo," she cautioned with a small pat on his arm.

Courtney shivered at the warning. Jared didn't respond, but firmly closed the doors behind Velma's retreating figure. The catch clicked into place.

Slowly he faced her, his tall figure and broad shoulders shrinking the large room. Most New York apartments would fit comfortably into a tiny corner of his home.

She squirmed in her seat, feeling at a distinct disadvantage. If Dylan hadn't been so comfortably settled on her lap, she would have faced Jared standing instead of him looming above her. The weapon didn't help.

As if reading her mind, he propped the gun in the corner, squatted down in front of her and stared unblinkingly at Dylan. The baby gazed back, still working on his biscuit. Jared thrust a hand through his short dark hair. It shook slightly and a flash of insight struck

Courtney. He may have gone all alpha on her, but their son had Jared King spooked.

Cautiously, gently he touched Dylan's leg, then clasped his tiny hand. The little boy grabbed his finger and squeezed. A small smiled tilted Jared's lips. A sad sigh escaped him and reluctantly he pulled away.

"Who wants to hurt our son?" he asked with a frown, his focus still glued to Dylan.

Despite some misgivings, Courtney had no choice but to trust Jared. That's why she'd come. She tugged a sheet of paper from the zippered pocket of the diaper bag and handed it over. "I found this pinned to one of Dylan's stuffed animals yesterday. Someone was in my apartment. They k-killed..."

Her voice broke as she relayed what little she knew.

He read the note and with each word of her explanation Jared's eyes grew icier. His jaw muscle pulsed. "Did you call the police?"

She shook her head. "I couldn't risk their

involvement with that note. I had to protect Dylan."

"I see." Jared stared at the floor, his gaze thoughtful. "Leaving was your only option."

His words were a statement of fact, not a question and the vice around her heart eased a bit. Maybe she'd done the right thing after all.

Who else could she trust after everything that had happened? Her entire body shook as her mind rewound yesterday's horror.

"I left Marilyn. On the floor. Alone. Her family lives in Maine. They don't even know what happened."

Courtney pressed the heel of her hand against her eyes to keep back the tears. The guilt tore through her. "I was so afraid they might come back, I went to my father's house. I thought I'd be safe there, but whoever did this knew I'd hire a car. The note warned me, and I believe them."

She'd never felt so alone.

On the drive from the airport, each time

she'd passed a police car, she'd considered flagging him down, and every time she'd let the vehicle pass her by. "I couldn't stop looking over my shoulder the entire trip here. I kept imagining every person I encountered was following me."

She clutched Jared's arm. "I won't involve law enforcement. It's too risky. He knows too much."

Would Jared agree? Was she being foolish? They'd killed Marilyn in cold blood. She couldn't bear it if Dylan... A stark shiver skittered through her. No, she was doing the right thing. She had to be.

"Hey there." Jared touched her knee and squeezed gently. "I understand, more than you know."

Relieved Jared seemed to see the situation her way, Courtney's shoulders relaxed, but only slightly. "Good."

"Courtney, do you think the blackmailer

knows who I am? Is he aware Dylan is my son and that you've come to me?"

"They can't know. *I* didn't know your name until a week ago." She bit her lip. She had to tell him everything, but if he turned her away… She let out a long, slow breath. "I only learned where you lived yesterday, but…" Her gut twisted and she pulled the cell phone from her purse. "They ordered me to keep this phone with me at all times. If they can track it, they know exactly where I am."

Jared didn't speak for a moment. Courtney held her breath, every muscle in her body taut with apprehension.

"There goes any advantage we might have had." He shot to his feet and paced, "Okay. Let's minimize your exposure as a precaution. Where did your plane land?"

"San Antonio." She rubbed the bridge of her nose. Why hadn't she thought this through more? "I should have driven, shouldn't I? I used our real names to board."

"It's not easy to get passenger lists unless you're with law enforcement or a hacker," Jared said, his voice calm and reassuring. "Most rental company cars have GPS tracking, though."

She slapped her hand over her mouth. "I didn't even consider that possibility."

"Why should you? One of my hands will return the vehicle to the airport, but we should still assume they know you're here and will contact you."

Jared settled across from her and leaned forward. "Let's get down to the real question. Are you asking me to help catch whoever wrote the note or do you want to pay the ransom?"

Panic rose in her gut and she clutched tighter at Dylan. "I'd do anything to protect him." Courtney avoided his piercing gaze. "The thing is, I could scrape together maybe fifteen percent of it, but I don't have the kind of money they want."

"They were very specific in their request.

Are you telling me that not only does the ransom amount hold no meaning to you, you don't have enough to pay?" Jared stilled. "I don't know much about New York fashion, but that's a very expensive designer dress you're wearing and the Waldorf doesn't come cheap. What kind of game are you playing?"

His narrowed look pinned her to her seat. She averted her gaze.

"It's not a game." She twisted the button on Dylan's clothes, struggling to ignore the suspicious tone in his voice. "I thought my father could give me the money, but his situation has…changed. Last week the bank ran out of patience."

"So that's why you're here." Jared stiffened and pulled away from her. "You don't need me. You need my money."

His tone indicted her, and she couldn't blame him. Most people would've been insulted and deep down the tone stung, but she understood. How many people had come into her life to get what they could? She'd learned a long time ago not to trust so easily. Or let anyone in. It was one of the main reasons she'd chosen not to live off the family money.

That didn't stop her from bristling at the accusation. "I came here to figure out what to do," she said. "I can't deny that you're the one person who can help me pay the ransom, but you're also the only one who has as much to lose as I do. I'm out of options to keep my… our son safe."

Our son. She'd have to get used to saying that.

Jared didn't speak for a moment. His reproachful gaze burned into her. She met it with unblinking eyes. Obviously he didn't doubt Dylan was his son. How could he? Their matching eyes were the tell. But the threat, the money, that could be an elaborate hoax. If Jared didn't believe her, she had no plan B.

She gnawed on her lower lip considering her options. There were none.

"We're not paying." The muscle in his jaw pulsed. "I refuse to be blackmailed. They'll just keep coming and it will never end."

She opened her mouth to speak, but he shook his head. "This is nonnegotiable. I'll do whatever it takes to keep our son safe. Giving into a blackmailer isn't the answer. I know—" His voice cracked. "Excuse me."

He quickly rose, scooped up the rifle and strode out of the room, shutting the door with a soft click.

Courtney stared after him. She wasn't quite sure what had just happened. She rocked Dylan against her, staring at the closed doors. Jared King wasn't what she'd expected. He definitely wasn't the suave man she'd encountered in the bar of the Waldorf, but she didn't need that man. She needed a fighter, and she'd witnessed the fury in his eyes.

For the first time since she'd walked into her apartment she felt a slight easing in her breath. Jared King was a warrior. A warrior with money.

A warrior willing to help them.

Whatever he thought of her, something in the set of his jaw gave her a glimmer of hope that Jared wouldn't fail.

She had to believe that. For Dylan's sake… and her own.

JARED SAGGED AGAINST the heavy doors of his study, his entire body shaking. The idea someone might kidnap his son… This couldn't be happening. Not again.

Though unlike Alyssa, who had been taken without warning, the threat to his son had put them on notice. He would do whatever it took to prevent the abduction.

This time, the outcome would be much different. Only one question ate at his gut. Was Courtney Jamison telling the truth. Was she a victim, or was she after his money? And how could he be sure?

He'd find out which, but it didn't impact his actions. Whether she was trying to play him or not, he'd never forgive himself if anything happened to Dylan.

The rest…well, the truth would come out. It always did.

Velma exited the kitchen carrying a tray. "What's wrong?"

"Someone's threatened to kidnap my son. They demanded a lot of money or they'll take him."

She gasped, set the tray on the foyer table and walked over to him. She pressed her palm to his chest in comfort. "This isn't five years ago."

"You're damned right it isn't. I'll be smarter this time." Jared shoulders knotted as he stood there. He couldn't meet Velma's gaze. He gritted his teeth. "It feels the same. I'm shaking, Velma. Like the moment I walked into the nursery and found the message."

"It's not the same. It's not *him*. This doesn't

have anything to do with you or your past. You didn't even know about the boy until she arrived."

"Maybe." Jared shot Velma a sidelong glance. "Did you see him, Velma? He looks like me."

She patted his cheek. "I know, boyo. No doubt about who his daddy is."

Jared stared at the scuffed toes of his boots. "I'm going to lose him, you know. Even if we catch the person threatening my son, Courtney won't stay. They don't belong here."

"Just because Alyssa didn't fit in—"

"Like you always say, the past is over." He gently eased away from her. "Have Tim quit messing with Angel Maker so he can bring in Courtney's luggage. Put her in the room across from mine. I want to be close at all times." The staccato words came out harsher and more clipped than he intended. He bent down and kissed her cheek in apology. "I'll be back. I have some plans to make."

He turned on his heel.

"Jared?" Velma called out. "He needs a safe place to sleep while he's here."

He slowed his pace, but didn't stop.

"Don't let the past rule the present, boyo. You'll regret it."

Did she think he didn't know that? Did she have any idea how tempted he was to grab that little boy and hug him tight. To take Courtney into his arms and convince her that they could make a city girl–country boy relationship work like a Hallmark movie.

Except life wasn't a movie. There were no happy-ever-afters. Not in his world.

There was only reality. And bad guys won way too often.

Determined not to let history repeat itself, he strode down a barren hallway. His first order of business was to take care of his son. He veered from the door of the brand-new wing he'd completed just last year and made his way to the end of the original house's hallway.

He hadn't opened the door separating the old

part of the house since he'd renovated, though Velma kept the place spotless. He stepped through, into the past. A white door loomed at the end of the corridor. His heart pounded, rushing through his ears. He forced his boots to cross the decade-old carpet to the end. For a moment he stood there. With a deep breath, he turned the knob and walked inside.

A never-used crib rested in the corner of the room. A yellow crocheted blanket lay abandoned on the floor. As his gaze took inventory of each item, one after another, pain twisted his heart. He would have bent over in agony if he'd allowed himself to feel. This room represented his failure to protect his family. And the threat that still loomed large over his life, a threat he would never deny.

He let his attention settle on a large hole in the drywall, marring the perfect paint job. A sledgehammer lay beneath the opening, a tool he'd swung with anger and fury and unrelenting grief.

Jared hadn't ventured inside the room in five years. He almost hadn't climbed out of the dark abyss after losing Alyssa and their unborn daughter. He couldn't go through that kind of pain again.

Jared would make it impossible for the blackmailers to harm his son. To do that, he needed to identify the person who wrote the ransom note.

Actually, it was more like a blackmail note. A demand before the kidnapping. Strange. Dylan hadn't been taken, but he could have been.

Why? What was the end game? To take a nine-month-old baby? To hurt Courtney? The more he considered the note she'd shared with him, the more he kept coming back to the unusual ransom amount. The number had to be the key.

He'd do whatever it took to find out who had threatened his son, and make them pay.

And then what? Jared closed his eyes. The

moment he'd recognized Dylan as his child, his soul had threatened to reawaken.

He couldn't allow it.

After it was over he'd send both of them away, back to the city, where they belonged.

And when they left, Jared had no doubt what was left of his heart would crumble to dust.

Chapter Three

A bright beam of afternoon sun slipped through the closed curtains and cut a shard of light across the study's rug. A few muffled shouts echoed from outside, but they were orders, not panic.

No way anyone could have followed her already…right? Jared was just being cautious. Exactly as she'd hoped.

Courtney glanced down at Dylan. The biscuit had fallen from his hand. He'd succumbed to sleep. At least someone felt safe after the last twenty-four hours.

She brushed his hair off his brow. "Oh, Jelly Bean. What have we gotten ourselves into?"

Her mind whirled with confusion. She didn't know what to think. On the one hand Jared appeared to be enamored with his son. On the other, he'd obviously felt used because of his money and had vanished out of the room as if he wanted nothing to do with her.

In any other situation, Courtney might have stalked out and headed back to the airport, but she didn't have that option. Neither of them did. Not when the most important person in their lives was so very vulnerable.

Dylan sniffed and turned his head against her breast. He snuggled in closer and she closed her eyes, just holding him.

Nothing could happen to him. She wouldn't let him be harmed. No matter what the consequences.

She'd already made too many mistakes. Whoever had threatened her knew enough about her habits to recognized that she hired cars from a single trusted vendor. They'd obviously been watching her for a while.

She'd resigned herself that the blackmailer would follow her and find her. She had no choice but to see her plan through.

A soft knock sounded on the door.

Velma walked in and set a tray down on the coffee table. "I brought coffee and cake," she said in a whisper, a frown worrying her brow.

The housekeeper glanced from Courtney to Dylan and back again. She shook her head slowly and clicked her tongue. "This isn't good."

Courtney stiffened, frowning at the woman who'd seemed almost too friendly outside. "I'm only here for Dylan. Believe me," Courtney retorted in a tight whisper.

"Calm down, dearie. I'm not judging you." Velma studied her with an eerie gaze, as if she were trying to peer directly into Courtney's soul.

After several moments, Velma nodded. She'd obviously made a decision. "You were right to come. Jared will protect you and your son, and he needed to know about young Dylan. It's just…" Velma poured a cup of coffee, and a bit sloshed over the side.

"Bother." She mopped up the spill, then gave up and sat in the chair opposite Courtney.

"I'm sorry for snapping. My nerves are frazzled," Courtney muttered. She chewed on her lower lip. Dylan shifted against her chest, and she cradled the baby protectively. "All that matters to me is him."

"As it should." Velma twisted her hands in her apron before raising her chin and meeting Courtney's gaze. "I'll say this only once, and we'll never speak of it again. If you hurt Jared, I won't let it pass. You'll find me a formidable enemy."

Courtney didn't know how to respond. She opened her mouth to speak and Velma held up her hand.

"*But*, if you are who I believe you to be, I'll stand beside you and fight the powers of hell to protect Jared's son." She clasped Courtney's hands. "I'm just afraid the two of you will break my boyo's heart."

Velma's unexpected words slapped Courtney in the face. "I'm not trying to hurt him."

"I believe you, but you will anyway. Jared might appear as impenetrable as a rock and too strong to wound, but he's been injured to the core of his soul. He sealed off his heart. You represent every dream he ever had and a nightmare he's barely survived."

The enormity of Velma's statement gave Courtney chills. "What happened?"

"It's not my story to tell." A marked sadness glistened in Velma's eyes. "Ms. Jamison, you brought trouble here. Jared will give his life to save you and Dylan without a second thought. Please don't pierce his armor. Leave him be. He doesn't deserve to be hurt again."

Before Courtney could process the cryptic words, Jared strode into the room. "We need a few moments, Velma. Alone."

The housekeeper left with a last pointed

look. Her words made Courtney examine Jared's expression more closely. She recognized the tension tightening his mouth and the worry in his eyes. But also a caution that she might have interpreted as suspicion before she'd spoken with Velma.

He sat across from them and pinned her gaze with his. "You'll stay. I'll help Dylan all I can, but you need to be honest with me. About everything. Deal?"

"I expect the same."

"That goes without saying." He crossed his arms, building a thick and solid wall between them. "So, who do you think is threatening you?"

She'd known he would ask. She wished she had an answer. "I have no idea."

His frown deepened. "You must have some theory. You have to have been thinking about it from the moment you read the note."

"Of course I have." She raised her voice slightly. Dylan squirmed in her arms and she forced herself to relax, lower her voice. "My life is simple and mundane. It's just me and Dylan. I can't imagine who would see me as an enemy."

He didn't respond but she could see the skepticism in his eyes.

"I'm telling you the truth."

He cleared his throat. "I've never heard of a ransom note *before* a kidnapping. Not to mention the unusually specific amount. Is it connected to your home, your family, your job?"

"The only numbers in my life matching over three million dollars are items from the gallery and my grandmother's trust."

Those words had him straightening is his chair in clear interest. "Trust?"

"It may sound promising, but it's not what you think. The money is specifically earmarked for the running of the gallery. Even the penthouse where I live is reserved for the gallery curator. I have no access to the money."

She stroked Dylan's arm and the baby's

breathing evened again. "There have been a few protests and threatening letters at the museum because of the Native American exhibit. The artifacts were collected during the nineteenth century, but the museum is in the process of returning the authenticated pieces to the original tribes."

"What are they worth?"

She understood the real question behind his query. "In total, a lot more than three million."

"So it doesn't explain the exact dollar amount." Jared rubbed his temple. "How about one piece?"

"I'll contact my assistant and have her look at the insurance values to know if any single artifact would match."

"It's a place to start," Jared said.

"But why would they threaten my son and kill Marilyn?"

"Marilyn was collateral damage, as harsh as that sounds. Dylan is a way to guarantee the money, but the amount *has* to mean something." Jared was silent for a moment. "What about relationships?"

The questions cloyed at the base of her neck. She recognized why he asked, but each query felt like an underlying accusation. "Don't you think I've racked my brain, gone through every possibility? And just so we're clear, I haven't dated anyone since I learned I was pregnant with Dylan. He's my only focus."

"And before? Maybe someone who didn't want to break up? A stalker?"

"I hate to go against the stereotype of what you see about New York women on TV and in the movies, but I was more focused on my education and proving myself in my career than in serial dating." Sarcasm dripped from her voice.

The more she justified her life, the more the fury bubbled deep in her belly. "This is getting us nowhere."

He winced. "You're right. I'm not a cop, I'm a rancher. We need professional help."

Courtney tightened her hold on Dylan. "Why am I afraid I'm not going to like what you're about to say? Please don't tell me you want to call the police."

"Not the police, but a friend. He works for a company called CTC. Covert Technology Confidential. They're local. I trust them, and they take…unusual jobs. On the down low. CTC has the expertise we need to identify who wrote that note."

Her entire body shivered. Were they really going down this path? "What if all the guy wants *is* the money? What if we gave him the money and he *does* go away? Wouldn't that be safer?"

"Do you really believe that?"

"I want to. I know you don't want to give in to blackmail, and part of me agrees. But the part of me that's desperate to protect Dylan thinks we should pay." There. She'd finally spoken the words aloud.

With a solemn nod of his head, Jared contemplated her quietly for a few moments. "I understand. But I have to ask this. Could you live knowing he threatened to kill Dylan, wondering if tomorrow is the day the abductor might come back with more threats, more *requests*? Or that he'll succeed?"

Jared's words were stark and harsh. She couldn't stop the chill settling at the base of her spine. "Of course not. I don't want to look over my shoulder the rest of my life. I don't want to be terrified Dylan won't come home from school one day. You see it on the news and wonder what you'd do if the worst happened to you. Yesterday the fear became all too real. It's a nightmare I can't escape."

He didn't respond, and she realized it was her call. She twisted her hands in her lap. Both were such a huge risk. "You really think your friends can help?"

"I do. From what I've seen, they have experts working for them that I wouldn't bet against."

She studied his face, his strong jaw. She recognized the determination in his eyes. She might not know Jared well, but something in that intense gaze, in the loyalty Velma had showed him convinced her to believe in him. She sucked in a long, slow breath. "Okay. We're in this together. Call them."

Jared gave her a comforting pat on the shoulder, strode across the room and picked up the landline. He dialed a number. "Ransom. It's Jared King. I need your help. And I need your word you'll keep it very quiet."

While he spoke to the man he'd convinced her to place her faith in, Courtney shifted Dylan in her arms. Poor baby. He was down for the count. She slipped his blanket from the diaper bag and placed it on the thick rug before laying him down. His face looked so sweet, so innocent. She shuddered at the flash of the memory of yesterday. She could have lost him. She almost did. Right now, she'd never felt more vulnerable.

Part of her wanted to run away from the

world, just disappear, but that would solve nothing.

A loud knock sounded at the door. Roscoe walked inside. She placed her fingertips on her lips and nodded down at the sleeping baby.

"The men have surveyed the immediate area. Nothing suspicious," Roscoe said in a low voice, eyeing her with skepticism.

His loyalties were clear. She didn't blame him. But she wouldn't allow him to get in her way, either.

Jared held up his hand and finished his conversation. "I'll see him when he gets here." He hung up the phone and turned to Roscoe. "Léon from CTC will be here later today. Make sure he has everyone's full cooperation."

Roscoe straightened, a scowl twisting his countenance. "Can I talk to you for a few minutes? Alone."

Jared gave the man a quick nod. He pulled out a Glock from the desk drawer and slipped it into his waistband. "I'll be right back."

They disappeared through the door. She had to wonder if he had a weapon hidden in every room. Right now, that didn't seem to be a bad idea.

"I don't think Jared's foreman likes me," she whispered at the sleeping baby.

Velma hovered in the open door. "Faith isn't Roscoe's forte, and he's definitely not subtle. He doesn't like anybody he doesn't know, but if he takes your side, he never wavers. He was foreman for Jared's daddy, and when Mr. King passed on, Roscoe watched the place until Jared could come home from the Army to take over the ranch. He's made it his job to keep the boy from working or worrying himself to death like his father. He'd do anything to protect Jared."

"And I'm someone who came here with trouble in my wake. I get it," Courtney said.

"You don't know her!" Roscoe's shout filtered from the other side of the house. "She's after the money. Just like—"

A door slammed shut and the angry words muffled.

Velma gasped.

Courtney's eyes widened. Just like who? Dylan squirmed on the blanket, letting out a small cry. Within seconds his lungs burst into a scream.

She scooped him up, but he had that I'm-not-happy-and-you-can't-placate-me-'cause-I'm-hurting look. She dug into her bag for the numbing cream for his teeth and rubbed some on his gums, then slipped him some baby pain reliever. "There you go, Jelly Bean. It'll be better soon."

Just as Dylan calmed a bit, Jared burst into the room.

"What's wrong with him?" he asked, his voice edged with worry. "Does he need a doctor?"

The front door slammed. Dylan howled.

Courtney winced. "He's teething. It's normal, but uncomfortable. The medicine should start working soon." She met Jared's gaze. "Is there a safe place I can put Dylan down for a nap? I think you and I need to settle a few things."

"About more than you realize," Jared said.

He glanced over at Velma. "See if you can't do something with Roscoe. I'll show Courtney their room."

"Old coot," Velma muttered, slipping out of the room.

With a sigh, Jared picked up the blanket from the floor and grabbed the diaper bag. "Let's go."

He led her down a wide hallway. She placed her hand on his arm and he paused. "Am I going to be a problem for your foreman? I could talk to him."

The tic returned to Jared's jaw. "He'll get over it." He nodded at a door on the left. "That's my room. You're across the hall."

He clearly didn't want to continue the conversation. Courtney would have preferred to leave it, but she had to ask. "If I'm going to stay, I need to know that Dylan will be protected."

"Roscoe's got a hot head, but he's never let me down. He won't now."

"Forgive me if I reserve judgment." Truthfully, the man's feelings didn't matter. She wouldn't be letting her guard down around anyone. Not until the blackmailer was caught.

"I wouldn't expect anything less." With a quick push, Jared opened the door to a perfectly decorated, perfectly neat and tidy guest room. Her luggage and Dylan's car seat sat in one corner. The queen-size bed dominated the space, but it would definitely do.

"There's an attached bath," he said, stepping aside so she could enter. "If you retrace our steps and hang a right, you won't miss the kitchen. When I'm not around, Velma can help you find anything you need."

Courtney entered the room. "It's lovely." She

pushed the comforter toward the end of the bed. Dylan still whimpered in her arms.

She sent Jared a sidelong glance. "It may take a while to get him to sleep. He's pretty fussy."

He backed away from her and settled in the doorway, with his shoulder propped against the jamb. She paced back and forth. Slowly Dylan grew limp in her arms. She expected Jared to get bored and leave, but he simply stood and watched her every move.

What was that expression on his face? Longing? Sadness? A little of both?

Once Dylan's breathing evened out, she laid her son in the center of the bed and slipped pillows beneath the fitted sheet on either side of him to create a makeshift crib.

"You're resourceful."

Courtney shrugged. "I can't take credit for the idea. The hospice nurse who took care of my mom used the trick to keep her from rolling out of bed."

"I'm sorry. Did you lose her recently?"

"A lifetime ago. I was ten. Brain cancer."

"Losing a mother is hard," he said, his voice laced with understanding.

"You, too?"

"Car accident when I was just a little older than Dylan. That's when Velma came to live here." He paused, his gaze focused on his son. "I guess we both know what it's like to live without a parent."

"Seems so." Courtney sent him a sidelong glance. His hooded gaze reminded her of that night at the Waldorf. She'd been sitting alone, not intending to speak with anyone, and when he'd entered the bar, her heart had skipped a beat.

He'd been everything she'd dreamed of in a fantasy. One too many drinks had given her the courage to sit on the barstool next to him.

He'd been wary at first, but something about him. She'd asked him a simple question. His favorite drink. The rest of that night they'd simply talked. He'd asked her about her favorite New York attractions and why. They'd connected about the important things. The importance of family ties, of honesty, of how they both felt as if they'd been born in the wrong era. How disposable the world seemed.

That night she'd felt...complete. For the first time.

She placed Dylan's favorite blanket on top of him, reassured herself he was safe. She shifted her weight. "I know we need to talk more, but I can't leave him. I'd be checking on him every five minutes."

"What if you could watch over him from the other room?"

"You have a camera?"

He returned a few minutes later with a small wireless device and pointed the lens at the bed.

After a few seconds he held the phone up to Courtney and an image of Dylan sleeping filled the screen. "Better?"

Courtney gripped the cell. After Dylan's

birth she couldn't count the nights she'd spent watching over him, terrified of making a mistake. Of missing something, of not being enough for him. She'd felt so alone. Eventually she'd worn herself out. That's when Marilyn had stopped her on the elevator. The grandmother of nine had held her hand and told her it was going to be fine. Courtney had burst into tears, and Marilyn had saved her sanity, agreeing to watch Dylan every day. From that moment until yesterday Courtney had felt confident that her baby was in good hands.

And now... Marilyn was gone, losing her own life protecting Dylan.

Courtney was alone again. Except for Jared, and she still didn't know exactly what that meant.

With a tight grip on the phone she followed him to the study. He gestured to the couch and she sat down.

"Before you start, I want you to know I was planning to tell you about Dylan," she rushed to explain. "I tried to find you when I realized I was pregnant, but the hotel wouldn't give me your name."

Jared grimaced. "They wouldn't give me yours, either."

"You tried to find me?" Courtney couldn't quite believe it. They both knew what had happened that night.

"I went out to get us breakfast. When I returned, you were gone. The concierge wouldn't say anything."

She flushed. "I thought you were sorry... Why didn't you order room service?"

"I needed to think. What happened between us was..."

"Unexpected?" she finished with a small smile.

"Very." Jared shifted in his chair. "My accountant forced me to buy that suit to meet with some bigwigs from a company who wanted me to sell off half the ranch. I hated that suit. It wasn't me. I needed some air to figure out how to tell you that the man you drank tequila with wasn't the man you thought."

She smoothed her dress. "I have to admit I was surprised when I found out where you lived, what you do for a living. When I met you in New York, you fit right in."

"Maybe for a day or two. I missed the sky the moment the plane landed," Jared admitted. "Are you disappointed? In me?"

How was she supposed to answer that? She could only be honest. It was all they had between them. "More like stunned. You acted like you belonged at the Waldorf as much as here."

"The tequila didn't give me away?" he asked.

"I wasn't drinking white wine, now, was I?" She settled back against the chair, foggy memories of the night filtering through her mind.

His hand touching hers on the bar. The moment he'd tucked her hair behind her ear and her breath had caught. The second she'd leaned into him and when she'd turned her head he'd kissed her for the first time.

The racing of her heart when he'd whispered an invitation she couldn't refuse.

Even now she flushed. She could never have imagined herself falling for a man in a few hours, and yet, she had.

He grinned, his eyes crinkling as the smile reached his eyes. "Hardly."

This was the Jared she knew. Quick wit, give and take. He'd challenged her that night, seducing her with something special, something she'd never felt with the men she'd dated. Only now did she realizing it was the cowboy in him. Who knew a big city girl could melt for a country boy the way she had. She'd wanted him, and she hadn't been disappointed. In anything. "I'm a quick learner," she said. "That was a first for me."

"Doing shots?" Jared raised a brow. "Or falling into the arms of someone you didn't know."

She winced at the truth. "Both."

"Me, too," Jared said. "We couldn't be more different."

She glanced from her Chanel dress to his jeans and Western shirt. "True. But the moment I found the note I was relieved you lived across the country and nowhere near my world. Dylan is safer here than in New York. We're both safer with you."

"I wish I were sure about that."

JARED LOOKED AWAY and the room went silent with shock. He hated seeing the uncertainty on Courtney's face. He hated revealing the truth.

She clutched the phone. "We are safe here, aren't we?"

"It's complicated, but we committed to being honest with each other."

From the moment she'd told him Dylan was in danger he'd mulled over the idea that he should send her and Dylan to CTC. Ransom had protected his location with the security of a military complex. They didn't know who they were dealing with. Whoever it was, they were dangerous.

He leaned forward in his chair, resting his arms on his jeans. "I've been having some trouble with the guy who owns the ranch north of here. I don't think he'd go so far as to drag you into our family feud, but he's unpredictable. Last week someone dug up the posts on a fence bordering the property. Several dozen of my cattle wandered onto his land. He's a loose cannon, volatile even. His goal is to drive my family off this land."

Courtney's knuckles whitened on the phone and she stared at her son's image through the screen, not meeting Jared's gaze.

"I have the sheriff looking into the vandalism, but the investigation is going nowhere."

His statement jerked her head up. "If the blackmailer finds us here, if he sees the sheriff—"

Jared held up his hand. "I'm withdrawing my complaint. I'll give the sheriff some excuse and deal with the Criswells on my own. Who knows, maybe if I back off, they'll get bored with these destructive pranks."

Jared was 99 percent certain the Criswells were responsible. He wasn't sure if it was Ned or Chuck or both, though. Ned had always been a greedy SOB. The bad feelings between the Kings and the Criswells had been going on since Ned and Jared's father competed for the quarterback position on their high school football team.

After his father's death, the feud hadn't died. When they'd discovered oil on the King property, the old animas had reignited with a vengeance.

Too much money made enemies of acquaintances as well as friends.

Jared should probably have dealt with the Criswell issue on his own in the first place. Too much like five years ago, when Alyssa had disappeared, he'd counted on the law. After the vandalism, he'd called Blake Redmond, who'd taken over as sheriff for his father. Blake had investigated. Ned, of course, had denied any involvement in tearing down the fences between the two properties. There'd been no proof.

There still wasn't, but the Criswells were the only ones who had anything to gain.

Courtney rose from the sofa, pacing back and forth. "Maybe coming here was a mistake." She turned the phone around, providing Jared an unfettered view of his son. The baby lay sound asleep, and completely vulnerable. "I just don't know. There are too many variables. What am I supposed to do, Jared? I don't have anywhere else to go. But I have to ask. Can you protect us?"

Her words sliced at his gut, much too close to the five-year-old wound that had never fully scarred over. This time would be different. This time he had friends who could do more than law enforcement ever could. He crossed the room, took her hands in his and looked deeply into her eyes. "I know you have no reason to believe in me, but I promise you, we'll get this guy. I'll do whatever it takes to make certain you and Dylan are safe."

She clutched his hands hard, her nails biting into his skin. "Whatever it takes?"

"Without hesitation."

COURTNEY FOUND THE intensity in Jared's gaze oddly reassuring. She unfurled her fingers and stepped back from him. "I believe you."

"I'll call the sheriff and ask him and his deputies to avoid the Last Chance Ranch for a while." He rounded his desk and picked up the landline.

Courtney glanced once more at the image of Dylan on the cell phone screen. Still sound asleep. She'd have to time his nap correctly or tonight would be a nightmare, and she couldn't afford a bleary-eyed day. She needed to keep sharp.

She walked over to the curtains and peered through the small crack between the light-colored panels. She didn't doubt that if she'd stayed in New York, Dylan might already be in a kidnapper's hands. Or worse. Within a few minutes she witnessed four men wandering outside with rifles in hand. The firepower made her feel better. At least for now she was safe. Dylan was safe.

They couldn't hide in the house forever, though. The only way to regain any semblance of a normal life would be to figure out who had written that note. Courtney knew of only one thing she could do. Review every person in her life to try to figure out who could be responsible.

Despite what she'd told Jared, she had to believe that somewhere in the back of her mind she'd seen something or done something that would point them to the person threatening to kidnap Dylan.

She pulled out a notepad from her bag and sat down. She'd start with the night at the Waldorf. The answer would come to her. It had to.

A phone rang. She dug through her purse. It was *his* phone.

Her entire body trembled. She picked up the cell. "Hello?"

"Did you really think you could hide by visiting your baby's father?" The sound of a mechanized voice chilled her to the core.

She gasped. No one knew about Jared. No one except the private investigator she'd hired.

"I know more about you than you know about yourself, Miss Jamison. You picked a man with a lot of zeroes in his bank account to sleep with. I'm sure on purpose. That's what all women want, isn't it? A man with money."

Her grip tightened until her knuckles paled with the effort. She motioned with frantic movements at Jared before tapping the speakerphone on. He hustled over to her and grabbed his phone from the table.

"You think you deserve what Jared King can buy you, don't you?" the inhuman voice taunted.

She glanced over his shoulder. Jared was sending a text asking if CTC could trace the call.

Keep him talking, Jared mouthed.

"Please—"

"Don't bother to beg. So, you discovered your father's broke, hmm. And now you're begging another man for my fee."

Courtney met Jared's gaze and she could see the shock in his eyes. Could he have been responsible for her father's financial meltdown?

"Well, time's up. Can't have anyone tracking my location, now can we? But, Miss Jamison, don't forget, you can't hide, no matter where you are."

A gunshot rang out from outside. Courtney's heart seized. "Oh my God. Dylan."

She raced down the hallway, Jared on her heels.

"Courtney, let me—"

She wasn't about to wait. She slammed open the door.

Her baby lay sound asleep. Her knees buckled.

Roscoe raced into the room. "Angel Maker's loose! He took down Tim and he's on a rampage."

"You'll have to corral him." Jared clasped Courtney's arm. "I can't leave them alone. Angel Maker may have caused trouble but he didn't get out of that pen without help. It's a diversion."

Roscoe gave Jared a frustrated look and ran out the door.

A diversion. Courtney strode over to the crib. A small stuffed bull sat propped against the side, not far from her soon.

She scooped him up and thrust the stuffed animal at Jared. "He was here. He was in this room."

Chapter Four

Jared pushed Courtney behind him. His pulse raced so fast his heart slammed into his chest. Impossible. The house was as secure as he could make it. The guest room had only three ways in and out. The door and two small windows. Jared gripped the Glock. While the orange-red setting sun glared at him, he checked the latches, but both locks were secure. He scanned the room. Nothing appeared out of place.

He searched the bathroom, under the bed and the closet. All clear.

"Dylan's not going to be without one of us.

Ever," Jared said, tapping on his phone. "Roscoe, I need a report. Where'd the shot come from? Was the shooter one of ours or a trespasser?"

"It came from behind the barn. I don't know who," Roscoe said. "Damn. All hell's broken loose."

Understatement of the year.

Shouting peppered the phone call's background. He could hear Roscoe questioning the others. Jared fought back his frustration. Normally, he would've been out there with his men, but he'd have to trust his foreman to take care of things. Courtney and Dylan needed him there.

He glanced over at her. She hovered in the doorway, poised to run, holding Dylan against her chest, her protection unflinching. Damn, she was brave. Their son whimpered and she jostled the baby in an attempt to calm him.

"In here." Jared covered the phone's speaker

and motioned to her. "Stay in the corner away from the windows."

She couldn't take her eyes off the small stuffed animal he'd tossed on the floor but followed his instructions anyway. For now, as far as Jared was concerned, this room was the only safe place on his ranch because he'd checked every inch.

"None of the hands fired," Roscoe said. "It had to be someone else. Frank said he saw some large tire tracks behind the barn. I'll check on it."

With an eye on his son, Jared mouthed a harsh curse. Criswell's F-350 was a big truck. Could the Criswells be behind this? "I want everyone on guard duty to stay at their posts. Don't let Angel Maker distract the hands if it compromises security. You got it? And find out who's trespassing on my land."

"On it."

"Velma!" Jared shouted down the hall.

Within seconds the housekeeper appeared

in the doorway, her chest heaving. "What's wrong?"

"Someone was in the house. He made it to the guest room. Did you see anything? Hear anything?"

Velma slapped her hand over her mouth. "Is Dylan okay?"

"The baby's fine," Courtney said, her voice husky with emotion. She pointed at the stuffed blue bull. "The intruder left that."

"Oh my." Velma sagged against the wall. "I'm sorry, Jared. I didn't think you'd—" She cleared her throat. "I brought that toy to him, dearie. I picked it up at the rodeo a few years ago. Since the little guy didn't have anything to play with…"

Jared wanted to sag to the floor in relief. The blackmailer hadn't penetrated the house.

"It was you?" Blindly, Courtney sank onto the bed, blinking back tears. "He wasn't here. He hasn't found us?"

Velma rushed across the room and patted

Courtney's knee. "I'm so sorry, sweetie. I didn't mean to frighten you."

No one could fake that response. Jared's doubt that Courtney had orchestrated an elaborate scheme for money faded to almost nothing. Which ratcheted up his concern. They were in danger from two fronts now.

He couldn't afford to make the assumption the blackmailer wasn't outside, not with the cell phone a homing beacon. The Criswells may have freed Angel Maker, but Jared didn't believe in coincidence either. The chaos that bull caused would make the perfect distraction for either the blackmailer or the Criswell's.

Damn it. Jared resented being under siege. With Courtney and Dylan so vulnerable, his hands wouldn't be enough. "Bring Dylan," he said to Courtney. "No one's alone until I secure the house."

He entered the kitchen. A large pot of Velma's famous Texas chili bubbled on the stove.

She hurried over to give it a stir before turning down the heat.

Jared opened the back door and checked the double lock he'd recently installed. "No sign of tampering." One of his hands gave Jared a brief nod. The man's rifle was handy and he stood at the ready with a good view.

After inspecting the front door, Jared headed to the cellar's steps, Courtney and Velma behind him. He made his way down slowly, cautiously, every so often looking back at the two women standing at the top of the stairs.

He flipped on the light. It flickered against the inky darkness of the root cellar. Light glinted off the small glass window just below the ground level. "We're vulnerable here," Jared said. "A man could just squeeze through if he kicked in the glass."

Jared studied the shelves holding Velma's canned fruits and vegetables. They lined the room. He'd never wired this room for security. Huge mistake. He grabbed a couple of two-byfours that leaned against the wall and climbed the stairs. After locking the door he jammed one plank under the brass handle and braced it with the other piece.

"That should hold for now."

"You think he's out there?" Courtney asked. "The man who threatened Dylan."

"I don't know. But I don't believe in coincidences, so until I'm convinced this house is completely secure, I'm not letting either one of you out of my sight."

JARED HATED WAITING more than anything. It had been over an hour, and here he sat at the kitchen table, his hand resting lightly on the Glock. Just across from him Courtney fed Dylan. At any other time, the picture in front of him might have made Jared smile. More food ended up on the baby's face than in his stomach. But he couldn't get the tight feeling from balling in his gut. The stuffed blue bull had been a hit, but whenever Jared glanced at the toy, another what-if ping-ponged through his mind.

Velma had apologized several times for not asking if she could give Dylan the toy. It wasn't her fault, of course. It was the blackmailer's. His note would keep them all on edge until he was caught. For now, they waited.

A too quiet Velma hovered near the oven. After a fight with bread dough she had two loaves rising and a batch of Jared's favorite cookies in the oven. Snickerdoodles.

The sweet scent of cinnamon and sugar wafted through the house. The picture should have been the epitome of a blissful home. Instead, the house had become a fortress.

Jared's leg bounced beneath the table. He'd rounded the rooms a half-dozen times, letting Roscoe and the hands take care of the pandemonium outside.

Courtney fought to convince Dylan to eat another bite of mashed potatoes.

"Jared never did like anything white, either,"

Velma said. "He'd spit it out. I finally added bacon bits and cheese and he'd scarf those down."

"Potatoes are boring," Jared said, willing to go along with Velma's attempt to keep things normal.

"Dylan's favorite is spinach." Courtney made a halfhearted attempt at a smile. "I don't know where he gets it from. I like raw, but not cooked."

A loud pounding rattled the back door. Jared rose, weapon drawn. Courtney and Velma froze. Dylan grabbed the spoon and shoved it partway into his mouth.

"It's me," Roscoe's voice shouted.

Jared inched open the door. When he saw only his foreman, he stepped aside. "What the hell took so long?"

"First we had to corral that damn beast. After we finagled Angel Maker back into his pen and calmed down the horses, I still had to figure out what happened." Hat in hand,

Roscoe limped into the kitchen and sagged into a chair. "Someone let the son of Satan out. Nearly broke Tim in two when the idiot tried to stop the beast, got me in the hip. I'll be lucky if I can get out of bed tomorrow. Frank's taking the kid to the clinic in town and I've got Lloyd watching the east side of the house until they get back."

"Did someone just waltz in and open the gate?"

"Oh, whoever did this was smarter than that. We found one of the pins missing. Could've been done anytime. Angel Maker had to hit the fence just right to take down the gate. Hell, the Criswells could've pulled the pin days ago." Roscoe shook his head. "That shot spooked him just the right way. This was way more than digging up a few posts."

Jared stared out the window, running through the last month and the last day in his head. "Maybe that's why Chuck was so jumpy today. He knew the gate could give way at any moment."

"You really believe letting the bull loose was about your ranch and not Dylan?" Courtney asked.

"Not everything's about you, city girl." The foreman scowled.

"Roscoe," Jared warned. "If the blackmailer wanted to create a distraction to leave Courtney and Dylan alone, he failed." Jared tapped his fingers on the table. "Right now, my money's on Chuck Criswell being stupid enough to fire that shot. Who else but a cowboy would use a bull as a weapon?"

"Sheriff needs to throw Criswell in jail and let him stew for a while," Roscoe said, frowning. "I bet he can take pictures of the tire tracks behind the barn and match 'em up."

Jared cleared his throat and met Courtney's gaze. "About that. Take the pictures yourself. I've asked Sheriff Redmond to back off the investigation for a while. We'll handle it ourselves."

The foreman let out a loud curse.

"We got a kid here, Roscoe."

"What are you thinking?" he said. "The Criswells will just keep coming. They could hurt someone. Or worse."

"You're right." Jared turned to face his foreman. "So, I want everyone armed until CTC brings in extra security. Identify who's willing to stand guard. Get back to me on the schedule. My highest priority is a 24/7, 360-degree view on the house. I don't want one foot in a blind spot. Whoever's left will keep an eye on our critical buildings. Have the men eat and shower in shifts until further notice."

"We've got stock scheduled for delivery," Roscoe reminded him. "If we don't meet those obligations we'll take a huge hit to the ranch's reputation."

"Send an armed contingency with them. If

Ned or Chuck let out Angel Maker, they're willing to do anything."

"Got it." Roscoe rose from the table, shot Courtney a sour look and limped away.

"I don't think he likes me much," she said.

"He doesn't like the situation. He likes you just fine," Jared said, locking the door behind his foreman.

She gave him an astonished look. Jared shrugged. "Well, he's just not all that fond of citified women."

"Citified?"

"That's one way of putting it." Velma let out a small guffaw and pulled the cookies from the oven.

"Life on a ranch doesn't always agree with city folks." Jared peered over Velma's shoulder at the cookies. "Tell me the truth, Courtney. It's hours to the nearest museum, symphony or even a traveling Broadway show. How happy could you be in a small town where the biggest excitement is a barn raising or the annual July Fourth barbecue?"

"Touché." She sent him a considering look. "It's not exactly what I'm used to."

Even though Jared had expected her agreement, it didn't stop the small pang in the region of his heart. Where was his head? He had to remember she wouldn't be staying.

So why did he have to keep thinking and hoping she might? And why did he have to like her so much?

She'd ignited something in him from the moment they'd met. A smile lit her eyes. Even in New York, something genuine exuded from deep inside her. He'd been drawn to her immediately.

She was confident, beautiful and passionate. He'd known that from the start. Now he recognized so much more. She valued their son over her own safety or comfort. Nothing citified about her love for Dylan. That was pure country.

"Roscoe has his reasons." Velma set a plate of warm snickerdoodles in the middle of the table interrupting his thoughts. "He met a girl in Dallas at a stock sale and fell head over heels. He brought her to visit the ranch. She took one look at the place and hightailed it out of here so fast her feet didn't touch the dirt. Kind of soured him. Not saying it's right. It just *is*."

The housekeeper sent a pointed glance to Jared. He knew what she was thinking. No need to mention Alyssa's first step onto the Last Chance Ranch. His wife had been shocked when he'd brought her home. Roscoe and Velma had both been skeptical, but Alyssa had tried to fit in. Prejudice went both ways. Jared would never know if she would've come to love the ranch like he did.

"No." Dylan closed his mouth and turned away from the spoon.

"He's finished." Courtney wiped his face. "I

need to change and feed him. Is it safe to use the bedroom now?"

Jared rubbed his temple. "More than likely, but I'm not taking any chances. Until CTC beefs up the security." He stood up. "Until then, I'll go with you."

Courtney stood and hitched Dylan on her hip. "You know I'll be feeding him, right?"

"He just ate." What was she talking about?

"*I* need to feed him." Her cheeks reddened and Jared realized what she'd been trying to say. "Oh, I see. We'll figure it out. But I'm not leaving you alone."

He followed her toward the guest room. He couldn't remember a time when he'd been more uncomfortable around a woman in his life. What had he gotten himself into? If he hadn't been terrified for her safety, he would have disappeared into the barn.

"Don't close the door," he said, planting himself in the hallway.

She nodded and disappeared inside the bedroom, shutting the door behind her halfway.

Jared hovered in the hallway tempted by her soft whispers and quiet laughs. He knew nothing about babies unless they were the four-legged, barnyard variety. Had no idea how long changing Dylan would take, much less feeding him, but he clearly was the outsider in this endeavor.

He didn't know how long he stood waiting when a flash of movement caught the corner of his eye. He jerked around, hand hovering over his Glock.

Velma jolted and raised her hands in surrender. "Dinner's ready. I took a pot of stew out to the barracks for the men."

"She's still with Dylan," Jared said, avoiding her gaze.

Velma gave a soft smile. "Have you held him?"

Jared cleared his throat. "He doesn't know me. And when this is over they'll go back to

New York. I'll be here. It's better not to confuse him."

"At first I thought you should stay away from her, too, but she's got guts, boyo. I like her." Velma crossed her arms and frowned. "A son needs his father."

"A child needs to be safe."

Tears welled in her eyes. "I know, boyo, but—"

Jared tamped down the emotion threatening to well from deep inside. He had to maintain control. He couldn't allow his feelings to color his judgment or his thinking. "I'm not taking any chances. Not with them. Not with anyone I care about."

"And that's why he won," she whispered under her breath.

NIGHTTIME PEEKED OVER the horizon. Jared caught a glimpse of the moon through the study curtains. He'd come up with a lame excuse to avoid Velma. Courtney had already found an ally in his housekeeper, but Velma lived her life wide-open. Always had, always would.

Courtney stuck her head in the door. "Are you busy?" she asked. Dylan sat on her hip and appeared utterly satisfied to be close to his mother.

Who wouldn't be?

She placed her tote bag next to the sofa and tucked her feet beneath her before letting her head fall onto the cushioned back. Dylan grabbed for her necklace and tried to stuff it in his mouth. Courtney played tug-of-war for a bit with him, smiling with an expression of adoration that made Jared's throat thicken with emotion.

The baby giggled and threw himself into her arms. She wrapped him in her embrace and rocked him back and forth. "Mama loves you, Jelly Bean."

"He's definitely energetic," Jared said.

"He likes to play, especially at this time of

night." She gave Jared a considering look. "Do you want to hold him?"

Jared stiffened and nodded to his laptop. "Work."

"You're missing out," Courtney said softly.

He knew, oh God how he knew, but if he fell in love…

Dylan wiggled in Courtney's lap and slid to the ground. She pulled out the stuffed bull and gave it to him. He threw it across the floor and crawled to retrieve it.

"Maybe he'll be a baseball player," Jared said, watching how every step or so Dylan would place one foot on the floor instead of his knee.

"He keeps trying to walk," Courtney said. "He can stand if he holds on to the edge of a couch or chair."

Soon, Dylan had situated himself beneath a wood coffee table and happily played with his animal having a conversation that Jared couldn't decipher.

Jared would've been content to sit and watch the baby all day, every day. He couldn't lose himself in his own wants. And he couldn't let Courtney and Dylan get to him. He had a job to do.

Courtney pulled out a notepad from her bag. "I've started a list of every person I can think of who I came into contact with since we met. I even added the car service. They can tell you who delivered the blackmailer's phone so CTC would have something to work with."

"That's a great idea."

Jared joined her on the sofa and glanced over at her list. There weren't that many names.

She flushed. "I told you my life was pretty mundane."

"Do any jump out at you?"

"That's the trouble. I can't imagine any of these people wanting to hurt Dylan."

Jared glanced at his watch. CTC should be here soon. Waiting had never been his strong suit. He preferred being in the middle of the action, and right now he felt more like a quail waiting to be flushed into the open and shot for dinner.

"How are we going to protect Dylan if we can't figure out who wants to hurt him?" she said, her gaze fixed on her son.

He understood her frustration more than she could possibly know. When Alyssa's murderer had never been caught, Jared had shoved aside any possibility of risking another serious relationship. He'd even tried to run Velma and Roscoe off, but they wouldn't leave. He couldn't understand why they'd be willing to take the chance, but they hadn't budged. Hadn't even moved to town.

For five years he'd prayed the man who'd kidnapped Alyssa would make a mistake, that he'd somewhere, somehow reveal his identity, but the man had vanished. The case had turned ice-cold. And unsolved.

Jared wouldn't let that happen again.

The doorbell rang, followed by a loud knock. Courtney jerked in her seat.

"It's probably CTC," Jared said.

Despite knowing the hands guarded the main house, he pulled his gun before walking to the door. He opened it.

Ransom's operative faced him. Jared couldn't hide his surprise. The guy could've escorted Courtney to a New York gallery opening or crawled next to Jared on the battlefield. His blue eyes were clear and piercing, with a decided edge that spelled danger.

No doubt about it, Jared would want Léon on his six, and not in the opposite camp.

"Rafe told me what you did for him and Sierra at the San Antonio Rodeo." Jared shook Léon's hand. "I hope you can help us."

"Rafe wanted to be here, but he can't leave Sierra. She's close to delivering the baby."

Jared could make out a slight accent, but couldn't place it. Didn't matter. If Ransom trusted Léon, so did Jared.

"So I heard." Jared led Léon into the study and brought him up to speed.

The man didn't take notes, but Jared had studied Léon from the moment he'd entered the house. The operative took in every detail of the room. He'd taken inventory of the gun case and the vulnerabilities in the study.

Of course Jared had clocked Léon's ankle holster, his sidearm and the knife sheath.

"Miss Jamison, may I see the phone you were given?" he asked the moment he sat down.

Courtney handed it over, and Léon cracked open the case. "GPS tracker. He knows your current coordinates—or at the least the phone's location."

"He implied as such on the phone," Jared said.

"He's smart and tech savvy." Léon snapped the case back together. "He blocked our tech from tracing the last call, so we have no idea where he is. Zane's working on a maneuver around the problem. He'll find it."

The headache that threatened earlier in the day intensified behind his eyes. "What if we take her and my son to CTC. Leave the phone here, and I'll answer when it rings. They would be safe."

"On the surface the idea seems plausible," Léon said, "but we'll lose our chance to set a trap. Without any leads we're thin on options until he calls again. The truth is, if someone wants you dead, they only have to be on target one time. To prevent him from attacking, we have to be on point *every* attempt. The odds are in his favor."

An ice-cold chill skittered up Jared's spine. From his training he knew Léon was right. Much easier to hit a mark than prevent an attack. If he had any confidence the blackmailer would leave Courtney and Dylan alone, he'd pay the money in a heartbeat.

Léon returned the phone to Courtney. "He hasn't tried to contact you again to give you a drop location?"

She shook her head.

"Interesting. What's he waiting for?" Léon mused. "It's more than just the ransom." He crossed his boot over his leg and tapped the leather for a moment. "If all he wanted was money, he'd have asked you for a million or two million, not that exact amount. It obviously has meaning for him, and that's his mistake. Once we find out how the number connects, we'll know what he wants."

Jared shoved his hand through his hair. "Courtney made a possible list of suspects."

"I don't think it'll help," she said, handing it to him.

"Every bit of information helps, if nothing else as part of the elimination process. Our blackmailer wants you to wonder about him. He wants you dangling at the end of his string as his plaything."

Jared ground his teeth in an attempt to maintain control over the fury ramming through his body.

"He's sending a message. We just have to decipher it." Léon met Courtney's gaze. "CTC is going to dig into your life and try to discover how that non-ransom ransom note ties to you. Are you okay with that?"

She nodded. "Whatever it takes."

"Whatever you need," Jared added.

Léon rose. "Until then, I agree you need additional security. Ransom will send several operatives to work with your hands. Now that I've verified the phone number, we can track the cell, and hopefully triangulate our guy's location when he calls you. And he will."

"So we sit and wait? That's your plan?" Jared frowned. "How about you take the phone and lead him away from here?" Anything to keep a distance between the tracking device, Courtney and his son.

"I hear you, Jared. Believe me. But he's got the leverage. He wants to communicate with Courtney, and we need to let him."

Courtney glanced over at Jared. He fought

against the desire to scoop her up, grab Dylan and take off to the mountains. Hole up in a cave for the foreseeable future. The Guadalupe Mountains were an unforgiving range he knew well. If he wanted to stay hidden there for months, he could. Instead, he gave her a slight nod. He might have a bad feeling about this plan. Anything putting her and Dylan in danger didn't sit well in his gut, but Courtney deserved her life back.

"If we're going to do this, how do we keep Dylan safe in the meantime?" she asked.

"I'll make sure neither one of you is ever left alone," Jared said.

"And we employ basic battlefield strategy," Léon said. "Establish a perimeter and no one gets in or out without us knowing. Then, we wait." The operative's eyes grew hard. "When he calls, Courtney, you'll need to keep him on the phone as long as possible. If it goes well, we'll be able to bag him before he makes any kind of move."

She chewed on her lower lip, but it was her white knuckles that told Jared how scared she really was. "You'll keep this low-key. No cops, no feds."

"I agree," Léon said. "Whoever did this is smart and organized. In fact, you need to take me out to the barn and introduce me to one of your stud bulls, because I'm supposedly here to negotiate a price."

Jared took Courtney's hand in his. "You okay?" She sent him a tense nod and he squeezed. "We'll make this work."

He walked Léon to the door and they crossed to Angel Maker's pen. The bull snorted.

Léon made a show of examining the animal. "This demon's got the perfect name. The devil's in his eyes."

Jared rubbed his chin. "You need to know I'm dealing with a saboteur, too. The sheriff was investigating, but I called him off. I think one of the Criswells took a shot to cause chaos. It complicates things. I'm worried about Courtney and Dylan staying here."

Jared didn't acknowledge his greatest fear. That he couldn't protect them. If anything happened to Courtney or his son, he'd never forgive himself.

"You were Army. We need intel. Right now that phone is our only link to this guy. Zane will start on the deep dive into her and her family's finances. Maybe we'll get lucky. Until then, we don't have a choice. Not if you want to find this guy."

"I know." Jared's jaw ached with tension. "Damn it."

"We'll ramp up your surveillance system and install cameras along the perimeter. The main yard and house will be secure. Your outbuildings, less so."

"But the best way to catch this guy is to follow the money." Jared walked Léon to his vehicle. "I don't like him holding all the cards.

We're like apples in a barrel waiting to get shot."

Léon opened the door of his truck. "Not for long."

Chapter Five

The day had been an unqualified success.

Stars blanketed the West Texas sky.

His prey was holed up like cowards inside the main house on Jared King's ranch.

She'd come running to Jared just as he'd planned. The note, the ransacked penthouse, her dead babysitter, they'd all pushed her into Jared's life.

Now, they were good and trapped and exactly where he wanted them.

She'd let Jared take her. She'd given birth to *his* baby. She would have to be punished for her mistake.

Oh, Jared had made the game a bit challenging, but a few hired guns would make no difference in the long run. The cameras would be dealt with soon enough. They had no idea who they were facing.

Money was the root of all evil. Wasn't that the proverb?

Except, it wasn't true. Being poor, being desperate, being without, losing every hope and dream, that's what changed a man. Made him into something less than human.

It was a hard lesson those barricaded inside the house would learn.

He would strip everything away, then they would understand.

They truly were nothing.

STEAM ROSE IN the bathroom and clouded the mirror. Hot water pummeled Courtney's aching shoulders and pounding head. Nothing could have prepared her for today. When she'd imagined informing Jared about Dylan, she'd pictured inviting him to her New York apartment, proving to him how settled she and her son were, how Jared could be involved in their life if he wanted to be, but that she'd be okay if he didn't want to be. She didn't need anything from him.

Fast-forward to now, and she found herself two thousand miles from home with not a coffee shop or taxi in sight, stuck in a ranch house complete with a killer bull fifty feet away, a murderer threatening to steal her baby, no money to pay off the threat, and her son's father glued to her side for the foreseeable future.

Even more astonishing, he'd never let any doubt stop him from protecting Dylan; he'd simply taken action. He'd done everything and more than she could've asked, including bringing in CTC.

Léon—he'd refused to provide last name—had been brutally honest, and dangerous. He'd warned her about snooping in her life. She had nothing to hide. Her father, she wasn't so sure about him. Since he'd lost the entire family fortune, he'd obviously made some bad business decisions or the bank calling the loans due in the last week wouldn't have mattered. Whatever Léon found out was worth a little embarrassment if it brought the murderer to justice and protected her son.

She just hoped they found answers soon. Her entire body throbbed with unabated tension. She could feel every nerve ending pulsing with pent-up disquiet.

If she let herself, she'd collapse into the tub in a blob of putty. Of course, that wouldn't do Dylan any good so she turned off the water and reached for a towel. There was no evidence the blackmailer was there. They had armed men walking the perimeter.

She had to believe they were safe with Jared. She had no other choice but to have faith.

The door was closed, but unlocked. On the other side, in the guest room, Jared had volunteered to watch Dylan, which might have made her nervous if Velma hadn't winked at Courtney and said she'd watch over the boys. Knowing the older woman would be within calling distance had been a bit of a relief. Enough to sooth the tension from her neck and back temporarily.

Courtney slipped into ivory pants and a soft rose linen shirt. Completely inappropriate for bedtime, but her baby doll nightgown would've been even worse. She'd been limited to what she'd left the last time she'd visit her father and what was in Dylan's diaper bag. Now that she'd arrived, she recognized she was completely unprepared.

A low, deep voice filtered through the closed door and Courtney cracked it open. Jared sat in a white rocking chair, swaying to and fro, his son in his arms, staring at the baby's face.

He toyed with the baby's fingers, counted his toes. She understood. The moment he'd been born, she'd done the same.

They didn't notice her, and she didn't move. She could only watch, stunned. Jared had avoided holding Dylan since they'd arrived. Now Jared's expression had softened into adoration, even as his jaw throbbed in stress.

Courtney recognized the feeling well. When she'd brought her baby home from the hospital, no one had been waiting for her. Panic had settled deep in her gut. Heck, she still experienced the feeling every day, usually after Dylan had drifted to sleep and she lay alone in her bed staring at the ceiling with the street noises of the city lulling her to sleep.

What if she failed him? Dylan had only her, no one else. The last twenty-four hours had exploded those emotions into heart-suffocating fear. She could hardly breathe; her entire body vibrated on the verge of tremors. Every horrifying outcome replayed in her mind like an endless loop, unwilling to stop.

Seeing the utter contentment on her Jelly Bean's face, for a brief moment she could breathe again. Dylan loved nothing more than being rocked. Especially if he were held tightly, and Jared, if nothing else, had a strong, firm embrace.

She knew that from the night spent in his arms.

The rocking chair creaked a bit beneath his weight until his surprisingly in-tune hum gave way to words. Courtney didn't know a lot about country music, but who hadn't heard "Mamas Don't Let Your Babies Grow up to Be Cowboys."

She rested her shoulder against the doorjamb. The only thing consistent about Jared since the night they'd met was the unexpected.

"You're not gonna want to be a cowboy, are you, Dylan? Not when you can be anything. I didn't have much choice. This dirt had bored into my blood by the time I could walk. You won't be brainwashed by the Texas sunset or the smell of fresh hay or the power of a quarter horse beneath you as you gallop across the summer grass."

"Sounds like a little boy's dream come true," Courtney whispered.

At her intrusion, Jared jerked his head up and grimaced. "In the movies, maybe. I almost lost the ranch until they discovered oil."

He slowed the rocking chair. "I think he's asleep."

"You can hold him awhile longer if you want to."

He hesitated then shook his head. "I shouldn't." With care, he stood and handed Dylan to her.

Courtney took the baby, expecting Jared to escape through the bedroom door and retake his place in the hallway where he'd spent the last few hours. Instead, he hovered, an enigmatic expression on his face. She shifted her weight and looked down at her son. Even in sleep she could see Jared, from the shape of his mouth, to the tilt of his head, to the slight smile as he slept.

"Léon didn't waste any time waiting for morning. CTC's men are updating the cameras and installing a perimeter alarm tonight. By morning we'll know if anyone unidentified sets foot beyond that two-hundred-yard point."

"That's a relief." So, they were safe. For a while. She needed some time. To breathe. To think. She wasn't sure what she'd expected from today, or this trip, but her entire body ached with fatigue. She needed rest. She glanced over at the bed. They would make do. If he'd just leave. "Dylan and I will be fine for the night."

She gave him a pointed stare, trying to get across the message.

"Where will Dylan sleep?" Jared asked, either immune or impervious to her insinuation.

"With me. I'll use the pillows. We'll be fine."

Jared rubbed his neck. "Would a baby bed help?"

"Of course, but where—?"

"I'll be back in a few minutes."

He left the room and his footsteps faded down the hall. When he reappeared, he carried a good quality wooden crib. Roscoe gripped the other end, the old cowboy's jaw tight with tension.

"The sheets are clean. Is over there okay?" Jared asked, pointing across the room.

She nodded, stunned.

Jared and Roscoe placed the crib flush with the wall. Before Courtney could thank them, Roscoe disappeared.

Still holding Dylan, she ran her hand along the smooth wood. "It's beautiful. I don't understand. It looks brand-new."

He didn't respond for a moment. His face frozen, Jared finally met her gaze. The pain in his eyes twisted her heart.

"Will it do?" he asked, his voice husky and so low she could barely make out the question.

"I'll sleep better knowing he's safe." She

placed Dylan in the crib and pulled a yellow blanket over him.

"Good night." Jared's soft words filtered through her. Before she could follow, he left, partially closing the door.

She couldn't let him leave. His words and actions didn't make sense.

She exited the bedroom. A passage of closed doors greeted her. Velma hovered at the end of the hall. She tilted her head toward Jared's room and then made her way to Courtney. "I'll watch the baby." She pulled a revolver from the pocket of her apron. "He'll be fine."

With a deep breath Courtney turned the doorknob. Jared stood, stiff, his back toward her. "Leave it alone, Velma," he said.

"It's me."

Jared's back stiffened. He didn't turn to face her. "It's been a long day. How about we call it a night. Please."

The rough tenor of his voice pulled her into the bedroom. With tentative steps she crossed to him. She placed her hand on his back. A shudder vibrated between them.

"How can I help?" She rounded him and looked up into his face.

He swiped at his eyes and gave her a half-hearted grin laced with pain. "A flash from the past. Just go back to your room, Courtney."

His voice pled with her to go, but she couldn't leave. She threaded her arms around his waist. For a moment he stood stock-still, stiff and un-yielding. She lay her head against his chest. His heart thudded, strong beneath her cheek.

Finally he slipped his arms around her. "This is wrong," he whispered. "I can't let you stay."

"But you want me." She had no doubt of that. She pulled slightly away and placed her hand on his cheek. "I know you do."

His thumb caressed her cheek, following the line of her jaw. He swallowed. "You are so beautiful. You make me hurt. I dreamed of you so many nights."

Her heart skipped a beat. She'd wanted to

lose herself in his arms from the moment she'd awoken in that hotel room without him. She called herself stupid at the time. People didn't fall in love in a few hours. They didn't know each other well enough to define whatever was between them as love.

A connection, certainly. She could feel the tug between them.

Before she lost her nerve she raised up on her tiptoes and pressed her mouth to Jared's. Maybe everything between them had been part of a dream? That night couldn't have been as amazing as she'd remembered.

The moment their lips touched she knew she was wrong. A flash of shock swept through her and settled low in her belly. She pressed harder, searching for a response.

What if he didn't respond? What if he—

A groan rumbled in his chest. He cupped her cheeks and his lips moved against hers, opening, searching for those memories.

He pulled her close, plastering her softening

body against the hard planes of his. Against her, his body trembled. Courtney clung to his shoulders.

This wasn't what she'd expected.

He pulled away, his breathing harsh and shallow. She blinked once, then again, still in shock at the intensity of her response.

"You shouldn't have," he said, his voice husky.

He wasn't wrong. She'd complicated everything. She'd been selfish, thinking of herself, and not Dylan.

He gripped her shoulders. "I can't do this to you, Courtney. In the end, we'll both be hurt. I know you don't understand why, but I *need* to keep you safe. From the present, and the past. I couldn't live with myself if something happened to you. Or Dylan."

Gently he stepped away.

"Jared—"

"Watch over our son. Please. And I'll watch over both of you. It's all I can do."

His body rigid with tension, he led her to the door. She had no choice but to walk through. Her entire body hummed with unfulfilled longing, but he was right.

Until they could be sure Dylan was safe, nothing else mattered.

JARED STOOD FROZEN as Courtney's bedroom door snicked closed behind her. His entire body shuddered. My God how he wanted her. He rubbed his face with his hands and cupped the back of his neck.

Resisting her might very well be as challenging as identifying who was after her.

He'd failed that night in New York. He'd entered the bar longing for a shot of tequila and to disappear in his room, get out of his suit and into some jeans.

Instead, with her first simple question, he'd been enthralled. She'd exuded elegance and sophistication until their conversation had shifted, and he'd caught a glimpse of her heart.

He'd convinced himself that their differences didn't matter. At least for the night.

Her devotion for their son, her fierce protectiveness. She obviously put him first. He admired the hell out of her. And that terrified him.

His cell phone rang and he looked down at the screen. CTC. Already?

"King."

"Jared, it's Zane Westin."

The CTC computer geek. "You found something."

"I need to speak with Courtney," he said. "And she needs access to a computer."

Well, hell. "We'll call you back in a few."

Jared ended the call and shook his head in disbelief as he forced himself to cross the hall. Was God laughing at him? He tapped lightly on Courtney's bedroom door.

She cracked it open, her eyes red, exhausted and emotion filled. "What could you possibly want now?" Her expression challenged him that any request better be important.

His brain went sideways, though, when his gaze veered down. She wore a silky, sapphire-blue, very short, very flowy scrap of material that cupped her breasts in a way that made him groan.

She glanced down at her attire and flushed bright red before disappearing behind the door and slipping on the shirt she'd worn earlier. It didn't help. "What do you want, Jared?" she asked, her voice tired and defeated.

He'd done the right thing, hadn't he? He was trying to protect them both from being hurt. Surely she could see that?

"Zane Westin from CTC wants to speak with you."

She buttoned the top up to the neck and closed the bedroom door quietly behind her. "You have the phone so I can see Dylan?" she asked, her chin held high as if she weren't half-naked.

He handed her his phone.

"We need to get on the computer," he said and led her into the study.

He pulled up a second chair and they sat side by side at his desk. He tried to ignore the flowery scent emanating from Courtney while the computer booted up. Hell, it took all the strength he possessed to keep his distance. He'd give almost anything to touch her.

She hovered beside him and he dialed CTC.

"We're both here and the computer's up," Jared said.

"Go to Courtney's social media page."

She logged in and a lively website displaying photos of Courtney at the museum and a few of a grinning Dylan greeted them. They looked happy and carefree. Courtney had created a good home for Dylan.

"I'm not sure I understand." Courtney clicked around the site, searching for anything unusual.

Jared had to agree. He couldn't decipher anything worrisome.

"Hold on. I'm sending you a link," Zane said.

A private message popped up and she clicked on it. The computer page shifted and a short text appeared. She blinked at the angry words.

When you play with people's hearts, they aren't the only ones who get hurt. Your time will come and the agony will come back on you tenfold.

Jared's shoulders tensed at the words. "Who does this guy think he is?"

"That's why I called," Zane said. "People say things on social media they would never express face-to-face. I need to know if this is someone who's just a hothead online so I can strike him off the list, or if you believe he could be a threat."

Jared turned to her. "Did he hurt you?"

She shook her head and he recognized the shock in her eyes.

"No, of course not." Courtney covered her mouth with her hands. "I never even saw the message. I didn't know I'd hurt him so badly."

"Who is he?"

"Desmond Hanover. We dated for a few months a couple of years ago. He got very serious very quickly. At first I was flattered, but soon his real interest became all too clear."

"Sex?" Jared asked.

"Something far more seductive. Money. He was more interested in what he assumed was my trust fund not the gallery's, and a job with my father than me."

"So you dumped him," Jared said.

"He was using me." She shrugged. "He came by a few more times. I threatened to call the cops and that was that."

"Some men don't handle rejection well." Jared would have liked to teach this guy some manners. A swift kick down Fifth Avenue would've felt good.

"But most don't concoct elaborate blackmail schemes requesting bizarre amounts of money, and they definitely don't commit murder," Zane commented.

Courtney tucked her legs up under her. "What if I just call him and ask," she said.

"I've done a credit search on him," Zane said. "He owes the bank over two million dollars and is about to go bankrupt." The clicking of speed typing sounded through the phone. "The numbers don't add up to our target, but he's a good candidate."

Jared reread the post. "The guy definitely has some anger issues."

He sent Courtney a sidelong glance. "You look skeptical."

"I can't imagine him killing Marilyn in cold blood. He never did like to get his hands dirty. I remember him going ballistic over a little dirt on his cuff. Let me call him."

"What do you think, Zane?"

"If I can eliminate this guy through a phone call and move on to other suspects, I wouldn't argue. If we don't like the sound of him, I'll keep digging."

Jared handed over his cell phone to Courtney. Zane read off Desmond's number and she put the call on speaker.

"What?" a sleepy voice answered.

"Desmond?"

"Who is this?"

Someone groaned in the background.

"Desmond, this is Courtney."

There was silence on the phone. "Courtney? Courtney who?"

Jared lifted a brow. Either the guy was a great actor or he'd forgotten the last name of the woman he was blackmailing.

"Courtney Jamison," she said.

Desmond let out a small laugh. "Heard your old man went belly-up in the markets. Guess

I dodged a bullet when you wouldn't introduce me."

Courtney shook her head. "And thanks for reminding me why I dumped you, Desmond. Sorry to bother you."

Zane chuckled through the landline. "I'm putting a big red *x* through Desmond's name. Sorry I had to bother you."

"I want to help," Courtney said. "Whatever I can do."

"I appreciate the offer. I'll be in touch."

"Zane. How's it coming?"

The man sighed. "The fact that I just called you about a loser like Desmond is a good indication I've got doughnut holes right now. Courtney, honey, except for this blackmailer thing going on, you're one boring chick."

"Gee, thanks."

Jared shot her a quick glance. Her face had paled to almost porcelain.

"Don't you worry," Zane said. "This isn't even close to my toughest search. Besides, it's always darkest before the dawn. There's a light at the end of the tunnel, et cetera, et cetera. I'm doing the dive into your father next. No offense, but your dad's data looks to be much more interesting."

The phone clicked off and Jared shook his head. "Computer nerds are a different breed."

Courtney didn't say anything, just stared at the computer where an image of her and Dylan took up most of the screen. She wrapped her arms around her knees.

"Don't let this discourage you." Jared rotated her chair to face him. "They'll find him. They're just getting started."

"I'm afraid."

Her stark words tugged at Jared's heart. He stood and pulled her to her feet. "Come here," he said softly.

He wrapped his arms around her and she leaned against him.

A visible shiver went through her. "If someone hates me so much they'd threaten a baby, why don't I know who it is?"

Her voice caught in her throat. The pain of her words reached into Jared's soul and twisted, jerking forward memories of confusion and despair.

He didn't know how long they stood there, clinging to each other, holding on as if they were about to be torn apart.

She gripped his shirtfront and finally lifted her head. He cupped her cheek and looked down at her.

"Better?"

She didn't say a word, but nodded.

Her gaze met his. Her curves pressed against his torso. Awareness flared in her eyes. Her breathing grew labored and his own body grew heavy with desire.

No doubt the fire that burned between them eighteen months ago had flared to life.

"I should go," she said. "It's too much right now, you know what I mean?"

He stepped back, his entire being missing her closeness, leaving a bereft emptiness where only loneliness remained.

She crossed the study and at the door looked back. He could have followed her, could have probably seduced her with one kiss, one touch.

He let her go. She was right. It was simply too much.

Chapter Six

Dawn filtered between the slats of the blinders in Jared's room. He sat in a chair in the open doorway of his bedroom, rifle within arm's reach, and stared unblinking at the cracked-open door to Courtney's bedroom. She hadn't really slept. Every time he'd checked on them, her eyes had been open, staring at her son.

He hadn't slept, either. Not that he could have even if he'd wanted to. Memories of losing himself in Courtney's kiss warred with the risk. Even if the Criswells were arrested and the blackmailer caught, he couldn't let his guard down. Each moment of Alyssa's kidnapping played over and over in his mind.

He couldn't come up with a win for the long term that included Courtney and Dylan.

Short term…he had to find a solution. Throughout the night he'd tried to work out alternatives. Léon had been right. Jared couldn't send them back to New York alone; but they couldn't go into hiding forever, either, especially without knowing the identity of the murderer. Jared knew better than most how much an unsolved case paralyzed life.

Someone had better find a lead fast, because they needed a plan. Jared hated sitting there waiting for some lunatic to make the next move.

A baby's cry sounded from beyond the door, at first tentative, followed by an ear-numbing scream. Jared jumped to his feet and slammed into the room across the hall.

In the doorway to the bathroom, Courtney stood in all her nude glory. She was gorgeous.

She shrieked and whipped a towel around her naked body. "What are you doing?"

Fighting against temptation, Jared averted his gaze from her damp skin and walked over to the crib. Dylan stood in the crib, clutching the wood edge, his face twisted and red. The kid could use those lungs full force, that's for sure.

"Whoa, little guy, what's got you so mad?"

Jared turned his attention to the baby to avoid Courtney's tempting shape. Dylan looked up at his father. Huge tears fell from his glistening eyes. His mouth pouted and the crying wouldn't stop.

Jared slid his hands around the baby's torso and lifted him against his chest, then above his head. The shocked baby stopped crying for a moment and looked down.

"Quite a different view from up there, huh, Dylan?"

The baby screwed up his face.

"It's not working, Courtney." Jared could feel the panic rising within him. "What do I do?"

"He's hungry and wet," she said, tucking her towel under her arms. She reached into Dylan's bag. "I ran out of diapers last night and am running low on wipes. I need to get to a store."

"You can't leave the ranch," Jared said. "Not until we know more."

She crossed her arms in front of her in an image he would never forget. An absolutely livid expression dressed in a too small towel.

"Well, Dylan can't do without the supplies. Can we send someone? Maybe Velma or Roscoe?"

There was a more immediate solution. Jared sighed, knowing he had to take her to the one room in this house he hadn't wanted her to see. The room he'd entered less than a handful of times in five years. But since he didn't know what she'd need or what sizes would fit his son, he had no choice. "Throw some clothes on and come with me. Please."

She must've heard the strain in his voice, because she didn't argue with him, she simply disappeared into the bathroom.

When she left, Dylan reached toward the closed door and screamed as if Jared were torturing him. He tried bouncing the baby up and down. Tried flying him like an airplane. Nothing worked.

Roscoe appeared in the doorway holding his ears. Jared shrugged.

"I'm going outside to work on the tractors where it's quieter," the foreman shouted.

The baby squirmed in Jared's arms. He was ready to bang on the bathroom door when he tried one last time to lift Dylan over his head.

The hard crying stopped. The baby chortled and smiled. Jared brought him down to face height. Up, and a smile. Down, and a frown.

After a few more push-ups, to Jared's immense relief, Courtney appeared in the doorway, dressed. Jared handed over the fussy baby. He should have been pleased to give his son to her, but the emptiness in his arms lingered. He enjoyed those chubby legs and belly, and that laugh. Dylan's laugh could light up any dark day.

"Let's go." Jared led them through the convoluted hallways to the old part of the house and the nursery door.

With one last look at her, he slipped the key in the lock and opened the room.

Courtney gasped.

He knew why. She saw a finished nursery with a few missing pieces and one huge hole in the wall. A changing table sat on one side of the room. The crib and rocking chair he'd delivered yesterday were gone. The walls had been painted yellow in a Noah's Ark theme, though the missing drywall marred the happy color.

Deliberately avoiding the scar, he opened several drawers and stood back. "Take what you need."

Her steps tentative, Courtney leaned over

and looked in the drawers. Dylan balanced on her hip, she pulled out a few onesies. "These are for a newborn. Too small."

Jared cleared his throat. "Try the closet."

She slid open the door and viewed stacks of cloth diapers and washcloths which sat untouched.

"Who—?"

"Take what you need." Jared picked up the never-used diaper bag and handed it to her. He knew each word was clipped and angry, but every moment in this room sent a tsunami of pain through him.

Courtney balanced Dylan and filled up the bag. The baby whimpered, then let out a full cry.

"I need to change him."

She lay the baby on the table and covered his midsection with a washcloth.

"Where are the pins," she muttered, wrestling with the square cotton diaper.

Jared's mind had gone numb, but he forced

himself to look. He dug into a drawer and pulled out some animal-styled fasteners.

"Not quite a disposable," she said, holding Dylan down with one hand. "I'm learning more and more to appreciate stick-on tape."

Dylan grinned up at her. He bounced with a laugh, kicking his feet in the air and sending the washcloth flying.

"You're an exhibitionist, Jelly Bean," she chuckled before fastening the last pin. She looked over at Jared. "Are there any rubber pants in the closet that would fit him?"

Jared scanned the room. He remembered storing a ton of unidentifiable supplies after Alyssa had gone crazy in the baby store. She'd bought items for up to a year old. He squatted down and opened the bottom drawer.

"How about these?" He handed her two plastic-looking briefs.

Courtney took them. "Even an extra. We should be fine for a while."

Good. Then maybe he wouldn't have to

come back here. He fought to breathe against the suffocating flood of memories. "I'll send one of the hands to Carder for whatever you need. Or better yet, maybe have someone from CTC buy what you need. Less cause for talk."

"Who would care?"

"There's no superstore in Carder. Just a general store. Everyone knows everyone's business. If someone from the ranch starts buying baby supplies, the entire town will know by lunch."

"I can't imagine having that many people interested in what I do or say."

"Small towns," Jared said. "Not a lot of distractions."

Courtney lifted Dylan. "I noticed a few toys in the back. Can I bring some with me? We left in a hurry."

"Take whatever you want," he said in a rushed voice. The room had begun to close around him.

Courtney piled a ball, some blocks and a

stack of brightly colored rings in the large bag. She paused at the two-foot-diameter hole in the wall Jared had been avoiding staring at since they entered the room.

"Let's go," he said, and lifted the bag over his shoulder before she could ask about the center of the wall he'd destroyed with a sledge-hammer.

With a slight hesitation and one last regretful stare, they walked back to her bedroom.

He braced himself for the question, because he didn't want to tell her. Didn't want her to know how badly he'd failed.

She sat Dylan on the rug and rolled the ball to him. He giggled and stuffed the edge in his mouth.

"Whose nursery was that?" she asked.

A DEAFENING SILENCE engulfed the bedroom. Courtney had been shocked by a lot of events over the last few days, but finding a fully stocked nursery in Jared King's house confused her as much as anything.

Dylan banged a ball on the floor, obviously enjoying his new toy almost as much as the stuffed bull Velma had given him. Courtney smiled at her son, but the expression faded when she saw Jared's devastated face.

Obviously the Last Chance Ranch hid a lot of painful secrets.

Jared stood quiet and unnaturally still, staring at their son with an intensity that made Courtney shiver.

She closed her eyes. She'd been so relieved to find supplies that Dylan could use, she hadn't really thought what it meant until they'd returned. She shouldn't have asked. How could she take it back?

"You asked about the nursery—"

"Everyone has a right to some secrets, Jared." Courtney tried to give him an out. The pain in his eyes was hard to look at.

"You more than anyone have a right to know."

Dylan crawled across the floor and pushed the ball at Jared's feet. It bounced against his boot and the baby grinned. Jared hunkered down and returned the ball to his son.

"I was married before."

She'd known. His wife had died. That much her private investigator had told her. As he spoke, Courtney wished she could retract the question. She didn't like the direction her mind took her.

"You don't have to—"

Dylan shoved the ball back at his father. Jared sat on the floor and focused on the game, avoiding Courtney's gaze.

"You remind me of Alyssa a bit," he said finally. "You both exude class when you walk into a room. You both look out of place on a working ranch."

Jared turned the ball over and over in his

hand until Dylan grabbed for it. He let the baby take the toy.

"We were happy. Mostly. But she got bored with small town life. We hoped having a family would fix the problem." Jared shrugged. "It might have. I'll never know."

He glanced over at the baby's bed. "I made the crib for our daughter. I spent weeks wanting it to be perfect. She never slept in it. She died with Alyssa."

Courtney couldn't stop the choked sob from escaping. He'd lost his wife, and his unborn child. She couldn't imagine the agony. She crawled to Jared's side and placed her hand on his arm. "Please, don't relive any more. I'm so sorry I asked."

He didn't move away from her. Instead, he lay his hand on hers and after a few moments lifted his gaze to hers. She'd never witnessed so much pain behind a man's eyes. He broke her heart.

"It's important you hear this," he said after

a long, deep breath. "I was busy trying to keep us out of bankruptcy. We couldn't afford enough help so I drove the cattle to the far end of the ranch to graze. Took me a day and night on horseback. When I got back Alyssa was gone. There was a message painted on the wall of the nursery. They wanted money in exchange for her safe return."

Courtney shivered at the similarity. "You've been through this before? Like me?"

"Not like you. I had no warning. When I came home, Alyssa had simply vanished. I didn't receive a note. The message was spray painted on the wall of the nursery I'd just finished painting."

Nausea rose to her throat. Please no. Not that.

"The guy knew exactly how much would break me. But he didn't know I'd just used all my cash to purchase a new stud. No way I could liquidate by his deadline so I called the local sheriff. I told myself I had no choice."

Jared's tone went flat. "The guy taunted me, made me think I could save Alyssa. I didn't follow his instructions and she paid the price. She died along with our unborn daughter."

Courtney leaned up against him and slipped her hand into his. "Did they catch him?"

Jared rubbed the back of his neck. "After it was over the guy vanished. He's still out there somewhere." Jared sent her a quiet, devastating glance that tore her up inside. "Even if we catch the blackmailer, the threat against me will still be out there. I can't risk anyone else getting hurt because of me."

What could Courtney say? She'd do the same thing. For a few moments, she rested against Jared, wanting him to feel her support. Nothing could be said to comfort him. A little human contact was all she could offer.

Across from them, Dylan gripped the ball. He pressed one of the sides and tinny music started to play. He giggled and rolled over toward them, shoving the toy at his father.

Jared's jaw throbbed and Courtney realized how much he strained to maintain control. She could see he wanted to let himself open up to their son. She understood more than ever why he couldn't.

"I'm so sorry for what you've lost. If I'd known—"

"You would've come here anyway because you'd do whatever it takes to protect Dylan."

Yes. He understood like no one else in the world ever could or would. "You're right."

"So would I."

The stark words reignited the connection between them. She wanted to say more, to help him, but she had no idea how.

Before she could work up the courage, Jared's phone sounded. He rose, relief written on his face at the distraction. Courtney had to agree, though she missed the warmth of his touch. Jared had faced and lost more than she could ever imagine. Nothing she could ever say or do would make it better.

"King," he said into the phone. Within a few seconds he tapped the speakerphone. "It's Léon."

"Miss Jamison?" The operative's voice sounded very solemn, causing her stomach to knot a bit. "Did you hire a private investigator to look into Jared's life and finances?" The rustle of papers shuffling reached through the phone. "A man by the name of Joe Botelli?"

Her gaze flew to Jared's. A cloud of fury darkened his expression. "Why would you do that?"

She swallowed deeply. "When I recognized you on the television, I needed to know who you were, Jared," she blurted out, knowing how the facts must appear to Jared. She would've taken it the same way. "You were his father, but I knew nothing about you. It was never about money. I had to protect Dylan."

Jared's expression had frozen into a mask. "Go on, Léon. Does he have any insight?"

"I'm at your front door," the accented voice said. "I think we should talk face-to-face."

The doorbell rang. Courtney scooped up Dylan and his toy, and sidled up beside Jared. "I wasn't trying to find out your bank balance." The words raced out. "You have to believe me. I needed to know if contacting you was the right thing to do for Dylan."

Jared rubbed his temple. "I get it. I really do."

Did he, though? Had contacting Botelli ruined the trust between them so soon?

Velma reached the door before them. She hesitated. "Should I open it?"

"It's CTC," he said.

Léon walked into the house, his face solemn. "We need to talk."

"Maybe I should watch the baby?" Velma said, holding out her arms.

Courtney hesitated. Every instinct in her screamed to keep Dylan tight in her arms.

"Are the perimeter alarm and cameras active?" Jared asked.

"Done," Léon said. "And we're constantly monitoring."

"It's up to you, Courtney."

She glanced at the operative's intense expression. He gave her a curt nod. "I think it's best."

With reluctance she handed over Dylan. Velma patted her hand. "Don't worry. I'll be right in the kitchen giving him a cookie. If I hear anything strange, I'll hightail it right back to you."

Courtney nodded and followed Jared and Léon into the study. "What's wrong?"

"You may want to sit down," Léon said.

"Just tell me."

"Botelli's dead. He was mugged two days ago around three in the afternoon near his office."

Courtney slapped her hand over her mouth.

"That can't be. We met at lunchtime in a coffee shop just near there."

"Whoa. Hold it. Mugged?" Jared paced back and forth and finally came to rest toe-to-toe with Léon. "Coincidence?"

A dismissive huff escaped the operative. "That's what the murderer wants the police to think. I'm not seeing a lot of investigation going into it, but I don't buy it. He was a Marine. Tough SOB from what I hear. No small-time punk took him out. Not from what I can tell. I have our forensic expert pulling the preliminary autopsy report."

"You can do that?" Courtney asked.

"CTC can do a lot of things. We have friends who owe us. They believe in paying it forward."

Léon took a seat next to the coffee table. "Sit down. Both of you. There's more."

Courtney couldn't imagine how much more there could be. Her mind had gone numb. First

Marilyn. Now this. Who had them in their crosshairs?

She sat down on the sofa and Jared settled in next to her, leaving a good two feet between them.

"This is a copy of Botelli's file on you, Jared. Nothing shocking. A few articles, financials, information about your wife." The CTC rep placed a folder on the table. "We have to assume whoever is after your son has this information, as well."

Jared glanced at the pages. She could read the fury in his glare along with a we'll-talk-about-this-later message. "Are you saying Dylan's kidnapping is because he's my son?"

"I started in that direction. Until we found this." Léon lay two more files in front of them.

Courtney glanced at the name on the folders. "Me and my father?"

Léon cleared his throat. "Some of this is a bit intrusive, but it couldn't be helped."

"Go ahead," she said, bracing herself. Her

father had shocked her already when he'd re-vealed he'd lost their family fortune. She didn't think she could be any more surprised.

"Your net worth isn't anywhere near enough to pay the ransom since you don't own the penthouse where you live. Your grandmother's trust is tied up, as well. Anyone wanting you to pay a ransom could figure out those facts easily and know they'd have to go elsewhere for the money."

"To me?" Jared asked.

"You aren't the first obvious source of money. Ms. Jamison is." Léon opened up her father's folder. A long list of numbers ap-peared.

"These are your father's most recent loan re-quests and lines of credit. All rescinded within the last week, by the way, which forced him to sell everything. He's broke. Take a look."

She winced. She'd hope her father had been exaggerating, but the evidence didn't lie. "There are some large numbers here, but none of them match the number in the note," Courtney said.

"We haven't found the correlation yet, but our current hypothesis is that your father's finances might be at the root of the ransom."

She sagged against the sofa's back. "Someone's using my son to get back at my father? Why?"

"We don't have the details. Not yet. Zane's working the issue." Léon met Courtney's gaze. "We're headed back east to see your father. We think we might get answers more quickly in person. And Zane can dive into his computers."

"I should come with you," Courtney said. "He'll talk to me."

Jared shot to his feet. "No way. The guy murdered an ex-Marine in New York. You're not going anywhere near that place."

"I agree," Léon said. "I don't even want you to call him. I'd like to see his face when I ask the question. Once we correlate the money to something specific, we'll be able to narrow down the list of suspects. We won't be shooting blind in our protection."

"I didn't tell him what was happening. The note warned me."

"You may have saved his life. Joe Botelli had opened a file on your father. That could be why he was eliminated."

Stunned was too limp a word to describe Courtney's emotions. "What about you and your team? Will you be putting yourselves at risk if you talk to my father?"

"That's our job. And we're better than good at it." Léon's expression turned cold and dangerous.

"Keep us in the loop, Léon," Jared said.

"And you keep your guard up," the operative warned. "You never know who the guy could hire, but my gut tells me this is personal and specific. That makes him less predictable than I'd like. We'll know more when we speak with Mr. Jamison."

"We need the answer soon," Jared said, and placed his hand on Courtney's and squeezed.

"There is one more wrinkle I should bring up," Léon said. "I left this one for last."

Despite Jared's reassuring touch, Courtney gripped her pants leg with a fist to shove down the foreboding rising inside her. "What is it?"

"The cops found your nanny's body, and they have your fingerprints in her blood. They've put out a BOLO on you and named you a person of interest in her death."

Chapter Seven

Today marked the second day Jared hadn't taken Mulligan for a long gallop across the ranch. He might not be able to take the quarter horse as far as usual, but with the cameras and perimeter alarms in place, he could at least stretch their legs with a walk around the paddock.

The ranch house's walls started closing in on Jared. He was going stir-crazy. He wasn't meant to be inside all day long. If he'd ever wondered how he'd do with a city job, he had his answer.

At just after noon his phone pinged a text message. The last of the alarms were in place.

Thank goodness. He picked up his tablet to view the new camera angles CTC had installed. He tapped through the live images a half-dozen times. He didn't see anything out of place.

Unlike his study.

Jared had to smile at the chaos. Dylan had littered the floor of the study with toys. Courtney lay on her stomach playing with him. They were in a holding pattern at the moment. After CTC's preliminary investigation, Jared was more convinced than ever Courtney's father was the key to the ransom demand.

They should know more soon. CTC's private plane had landed in New York and they were on their way to see Edward Jamison.

"Okay, I've had it," Jared said. He snagged his son into his arms. "How about you and I go outside?"

Courtney looked up at them. "Outside?"

"The alarms and cameras are up. There's nowhere the blackmailer can hide. The guards are on duty. Dylan and I are going down to the barn to look at the animals. We'll stay close."

The baby tilted his head and threw his arms around Jared's neck.

His chest tightened at his son's response. Dylan didn't have any pretense. He was so refreshing.

"Would you like to come?" he asked Courtney.

"I have to get something from the bedroom. I'll meet you down there."

Jared hesitated, but she gave him an encouraging smile. He could see what she was doing. She wanted him to bond with his son. Well, it had taken all of a smile for Jared to want more than anything to throw all caution aside and give the baby the world.

Every moment he was around Dylan he fought against those instincts. So what was he thinking spending more time with the child? He could blame cabin fever. Why not? It was better than the truth. That he wanted to get to know his son, his quirks, his sense of humor, what made him laugh and cry, what made him angry.

"This may be a big mistake, Dylan, but we're doing it anyway." He strode out of the study and out the front door.

The porch stretched to either side. Jared walked to the corner of the house. The men walking guard duty appeared shocked to see him with a baby in hand. Well, they'd have to get used to it. Until this was over. Tim was brave enough—or young enough—to approach Jared. His arm was in a soft cast. He smiled at the baby.

"Cute kid."

"How you doing?"

Tim shrugged. "Angel Maker just clipped me. I'm fine."

"You're not on pain meds are you? You need to be alert with that rifle at your side."

"Just some ibuprofen. I swear."

Jared nodded. "You see anything unusual?"

"Except for the bull going AWOL?"

"Except for that."

Tim shook his head. "It's been real quiet. Everyone's on guard, Mr. King. Nobody wants nothing to happen to your boy and your lady."

His lady. The words made his gut ache, but he forced a smile. "Get back to your post. The kid and I are going to explore a little. See if you can't find time to walk Mulligan a bit sometime today."

With a half-baked salute, Tim rushed over to the other side of the house.

"It's hard to find good help, Dylan. When I was about twelve, I thought I'd be running this place with my best friend, but he didn't love it like I did. He likes computers. Frankly, I'd recommend following Derek's lead. That's where the money is. Unless you happen to get lucky and a few dinosaurs died a million years ago under the dirt."

Jared stepped onto the road and walked toward the barn and stables.

"This is my ranch, son." Jared swallowed past the thickness in his throat. His legacy. "The Last Chance Ranch, because it was my ancestors' last chance at redemption for a few too many wild adventures. The Kings have been here for six generations. Mostly causing trouble. You're too young to hear those stories. Maybe someday."

Dylan tilted his head and patted Jared's cheek. He rubbed against the stubble and giggled before stretching out to try to grab Jared's Stetson.

"You're a cowboy at heart, aren't you, little guy?"

Jared's heart filled with pride. He'd never dreamed he'd be here, with his son. Courtney had given him an unimaginable gift. He leaned low and nuzzled Dylan's cheek. "I love you," he whispered softly. "You may not remember, but I always will."

He reshuffled his son and together they headed toward Angel Maker's pen. The gate had been fixed and reinforced. The bull Angel Maker snorted his red eyes staring down the baby. Dylan's gaze grew wide. He reached out a hand.

"Oh no you don't, my boy. He's dangerous. You can't go near any of the animals without me or your mama or Roscoe or Velma, but Angel Maker in particular. He might be a mean one, but his genetic material is going to create some excellent stock. You know what, kid, maybe someday I'll take you to the rodeo…"

Jared's voice petered off. That wasn't going to be happening, not once he sent Dylan and his mother back to New York. For their own safety. Until Alyssa's killer was caught, Jared wouldn't take the risk.

The idea made his gut ache. He shook off the feeling and pushed through the double doors on the horse barn. "See all that hay. That's what horses eat."

Jared chuckled. He didn't know exactly what

Dylan understood but that look on his son's face made him wonder if he wasn't horrified at the idea of eating straw.

"I'll give you a hint. Velma's cookies are *way* better than a horse's diet."

He walked down a row of stables. "Let's go see Mulligan. He'll like you." He walked across the hay to the stall where his favorite mount chomped on feed. Jared pulled out a carrot from the barn stash. Dylan reached for it.

"I don't know if you can eat this, little guy. I'm pretty sure I'd have to turn it into mush, but it's one of Mulligan's favorites."

Those big brown eyes blinked, then the beast looked away.

"Unless he's pouting." Jared reached over the gate to pat the horse. "I know, boy. It's been too long since your ride, and we can't go today. So how about that carrot?"

The horse didn't reach for it. Jared shrugged. "I could take it away."

He left his hand open and Mulligan chomped down the vegetable. "I thought so."

He patted the animal's neck.

"Okay, boy. Be still. We have a visitor." He shifted Dylan in his arms. "Son, this is Mulligan. He's my horse."

Jared gently guided Dylan's hand to the horse's soft nose. His son's mouth opened in awe and he patted the animal's fur, then turned a bright grin on his father. "I thought you'd like him."

The baby squirmed in Jared's arms. "You want down? Sorry. Not in here. Not until you're older."

Dylan screwed up his face.

"Don't give me that. How about we go see the tractor."

Jared exited the barn and rounded the building. A large green tractor was parked, waiting for a rider. He eyed one of the CTC guards and sent him a questioning glance. The man sent him a go-ahead signal so Jared climbed up and sat in the seat. "We're high up here, aren't we?"

Dylan rubbed his eyes and buried his head against Jared's chest. "Are you shy? Did I scare you?"

Had he done something wrong?

"He's just sleepy," Courtney's voice said from down below them. Tim had followed her, and Jared gave him an appreciative nod before the young man returned to his patrol.

She was gazing at him with an expression he didn't want to recognize. They both had to be careful. They shared one night and a child. Emotions and feelings had ruled one night. They both needed to keep their heads on straight for now.

"You're very good with him."

"Kids and ranches go together. There's nothing hard about it."

Dylan blinked and reached his arms down to his mother. She smiled. "You ready for a nap, Jelly Bean?"

The baby frowned, but Courtney simply chuckled. "I think you are."

Jared climbed down from the tractor and handed his son to her, leaving him empty. And not only his arms.

"I want to try to keep him on his normal schedule as much as possible," she said. "Even though nothing about right now is normal." They made their way into the house.

"I understand. But I'm still your shadow. For now at least."

"Are you sure? I'm feeding him again."

Jared's gulp echoed through the air. Courtney bit back a grin. They returned to the house to the bedroom and she settled in the rocking chair. Jared took his place just outside the door, but looked away when she nestled Dylan to her breast. She covered them both with a blanket and eased back and forth.

"See-saw, rocky-daw," she hummed softly.

Jared peeked out of the corner of his eye. She toyed with the hair falling on Dylan's forehead. Jared had never really considered the intimate relationship between mother and child. Even if he were part of their life, he could never have the kind of relationship Courtney had with Dylan. Their bond excluded him. Did other fathers feel the same way?

She swayed to and fro, her eyes closed. At least she felt comfortable enough to relax. The discoloration beneath her eyes revealed her need for sleep. The last couple days had been tough.

Her eyes opened and she met his gaze. "He's asleep." She fiddled with her clothes under the blanket and removed it. His son's eyes were closed, his small mouth slightly open in sleep.

"You're exhausted," Jared said, stepping into the room. "I know you didn't sleep much last night. You should get some rest."

She shook her head. "I wouldn't feel comfortable." She rose and lay Dylan in the crib.

Jared held his breath. If he'd learned one thing in the last twenty-four hours it was that

Dylan could go from sleep to awake in a split second. The baby shifted a few times, nestling down into his blanket, then finally settled on the mattress with the fuzzy blue bull clutched in one hand.

Courtney sighed in relief. "Another cup of coffee will hit the spot."

She veered toward him and Jared reached out his hand, stopping her. They faced each other and he couldn't breathe. Her eyes softened and melted his heart.

"You're an amazing mother," he said. "Dylan's a wonderful little boy."

She shook her head. "I don't know what I'm doing half the time."

"You fooled me, because I don't see how you could have done better with him." Jared tucked her hair behind her ear, just as he had that night. "The night we met, you said you longed for something permanent in your life, that wouldn't be disposable."

"And I got Dylan." She frowned. "I can't lose him, Jared."

"We're safe enough for now. Take a nap."

"I can't. What if I fall asleep and something happens?" She swiped at her eyes. "What's wrong with me? I'm not usually this weepy and I've been like a faucet since I arrived."

"No sleep and stress will do it every time. Believe me, I know. Lean on me. That's why I'm here." Jared pulled her into his arms and held her close. She rested her head against his chest. "Come to bed. I'll watch over you both."

She gripped his shirt tight and he walked her backward toward the bed. She let him push her onto the mattress. He knelt in front of her and pulled off her ballet flats.

"If you hang around much longer, we need to get you some boots." Jared rotated her legs on the bed and stared down at her.

She gripped his hand. "Stay with me." Her eyes were pleading and vulnerable. "I can't do this alone, Jared. I know you're trying to protect us from your past, but right now the present is scary enough. Can't we deal with one crazy person at a time?"

Her words didn't allay his fears, only reminded him of the threats. "I don't want you hurt, Courtney."

"Me, either. So, stay with me. Just for today. I'm tired of being alone in this, Jared. I need you."

The three words twisted his heart. He sat on the bed and pulled off his boots, shifting until he lay beside her. He pulled her back against him and lifted the quilt over them.

They lay spooned, facing the crib so he could watch over Dylan.

"Thank you," she whispered.

The room went silent save for their breathing. The heat between their bodies cocooned Jared in warmth. If someone weren't trying to destroy everything around him he would have said he was experiencing a slice of heaven.

He didn't know how long they lay there together, but he knew she hadn't drifted off to sleep. Her breathing hadn't fallen into that deep, regular pattern.

"The noises here are so different from New York," she whispered.

"No traffic, no horns, no impatience."

"I hear some muffled shouts and a bit of puttering around the house, but it's so quiet."

"Is that good or bad?" Jared whispered in her ear, trying to keep himself from nuzzling her neck. All he'd have to do would be to turn her toward him and he could kiss her. He didn't think she'd say no.

"I'm used to blocking out noise. It's hard to fall asleep without it."

As if she'd read his mind she turned in his arms. "I can't fall asleep," she said, staring at his lips. "My mind keeps dwelling on horrible possibilities."

She placed her hand on his cheek. "I want to forget, Jared. Just for a few minutes. Can you help me forget?"

HER ENTIRE BODY TREMBLING, Courtney clutched his shirt. Would he pull away from her? Her stomach flipped with nerves. What had she been thinking? Could she laugh it off, blame her insane offer on lack of sleep?

"Courtney. Look at me," Jared said, his voice low and deep.

She forced herself to raise her head and meet his gaze. His eyes had darkened with intensity. He turned her hand over and kissed her palm, lightly, gently.

Her heart thudded in response.

"Does that help you forget?" he asked with an infinitesimal smile in his voice.

"No," she said breathlessly.

His lips touched the top of her head. "How about now?"

"Not yet."

He shifted his weight and her head rested against his shoulder. His ran his lips along her temple. "Now?"

Courtney closed her eyes, leaning into him.

The pine scent of his soap intoxicated her. "No. Please."

His finger tilted her chin up and he kissed her cheek, moving along her skin until he came ever so close to the corner of her mouth.

"Jared," she groaned.

He pulled back and stared deeply into her eyes. His callused hand toyed with her hair. "It's like spun gold," he said quietly. "Almost unreal."

His fingertips followed the line of her cheek to her throat. Courtney held her breath, anticipating his next touch, terrified he would stop, that he would allow her to think again.

He simply stared at her, silent. Her body trembled in anticipation. He touched her lip with his thumb tugging gently, then traced her mouth, teasing the sensitive nerve endings until she wanted to scream.

"Please," she breathed. "Please kiss me."

"I dreamed of you," he whispered. "Too many nights."

"Me, too. Sometimes I didn't think it was real."

"Except you had our baby."

"And he's proof that the entire night wasn't all in my imagination."

"Are you sure about this?" he asked carefully. "Emotions ruled that night. I have a feeling they are again."

"I don't care," she said. "I've been waiting a year and a half to feel alive again. Don't make me wait any longer."

With a force that surprised even her, she tugged at his lips and he opened his mouth, tasting the salt of her skin. Courtney closed her eyes against the overwhelming emotions. For the first time since she'd awoken in the lonely bed in the hotel room she didn't feel utterly alone.

He swallowed deeply. "If I kiss you, Courtney, I won't stop."

"I don't want you to."

He lowered his mouth and his lips touched

hers. She wrapped her arms around his back and pulled him closer, wanting to feel his body on top of hers.

"Jared!"

Roscoe's shout tore them apart. Jared wrenched his lips away from hers and catapulted off the bed.

The foreman rushed into the room, his gait off-kilter from his earlier encounter with Angel Maker. "A brush fire popped up from the north near the oil rigs. It's been dry the last few months and we've got a twenty-mile-an-hour wind. It's heading for the quarter horse facility."

JARED GRABBED HIS boots and sat on the edge of the bed. He refused to look at Courtney. He could imagine the invitation on her swollen lips and passion-filled eyes.

Dylan whimpered and stood up in his crib. Courtney crossed to him and whispered to him, calming the baby.

"Lightning?" Jared asked, facing Roscoe. He didn't appreciate the arch of a brow on his foreman's face.

He shoved his feet into his boots. Roscoe didn't say a word, only tossed his shoulder holster at him.

So much for being discrete. Roscoe knew exactly what they'd been about to do.

"No storms, no clouds. It came out of nowhere."

"Man-made, then. Could be an accident. Could be one of the Criswells." Jared strode across the hall and grabbed his rifle. "Velma!"

At his call, the housekeeper rushed into the bedroom. He handed her the weapon and gave Courtney the keys to his truck. "Stay locked in this room with Dylan. If the fire gets out of control, I'll call and you two head for CTC. Velma knows where it is. Got it?"

The housekeeper pointed the barrel toward the ground and nodded. Courtney gripped the keys tight.

Jared tried to give her a confident smile. "It's part of living in the middle of nowhere. You gotta do for yourself. By the time the volunteer fire truck arrives, we'll have this thing out. Right, Roscoe?"

"Sure, Jared." The foreman studied Velma, his features looked pale and nauseous. "You don't take any chances, woman. You hear me?"

"Oh, quit your sweet talkin'. Besides, maybe one of the hands flipped a cigarette," Velma said, the perpetual Pollyanna. "Some of 'em got no more sense than a bullfrog."

Roscoe stared at her like she was crazy.

"It could be," she protested.

"Get your head out of the dirt, woman. You know what's happened. Criswell is upping his threat. He's trying to force Jared to give in."

"There is another option," Courtney said. "What if it's *him*? What if he's here, on this ranch."

Jared thrust his hand through his hair. "We'll

review the video footage after we take care of the fire. In the meantime, do what you have to do to protect yourself," he ordered. "I'll leave as many men to guard you as I can. The CTC operatives are out there and I'll make certain more are on the way. You're not alone." He sent Velma a stern look. "Just don't shoot me on the way back in."

"Get out of here, boyo," Velma said. "We women can take care of ourselves. Been doing it all my life."

She gripped the rifle with the very determined look on her face he recognized so well. She would do whatever it took to protect her family. So would Courtney.

Jared paused, then pulled her close and gave her a hard kiss on the lips. "You take care of our son. I'll be back soon."

He took one last look at his unhappy son before racing out of the room. Roscoe headed for the truck and Jared locked the door behind them. He took in a quick sweep of the guards.

"No one gets in that house except me or Roscoe," he ordered.

They nodded. Angel Maker snorted in his pen as if in agreement. Crazy bull.

"Let's go," Jared shouted and jumped into his truck. Several hands leaped into the back. Jared pushed the truck as fast as he could, heading north. He could see the smoke rising. There was a lot of it.

Once or twice, though, he caught himself glancing in the rearview mirror. "I don't like leaving them," he said to Roscoe.

"Get your head in the game, Jared. If the fire gets past those buildings, the wind'll bring it to the house way fast. The whole place will go up in flames, and we might not be able to get back in time," Roscoe said. "We gotta stop it up here."

The truth of his foreman's words chilled Jared. As they got closer thick smoke settled on the air making it tough to breathe.

"Break out the masks the minute I stop," he said.

"The men know what to do," Roscoe said. "I trained 'em. And you. So let them do their job."

Jared skidded to a stop a few hundred feet from the barns. He looked on in horror. The crackling fire had licked its way up the backside of the large structure.

Roscoe exited the truck and started shouting orders. The men piled out of the vehicle and grabbed a pile of white smoke masks. They weren't anything like what firefighters wore, but they'd keep their lungs clear in the short term.

An explosion made the ground shudder. Thick smoke billowed from the top of the barn. Okay, that wasn't normal.

Jared tapped his phone to speed dial CTC.

"What's going on out there, Jared?" Ransom asked. "I got an emergency page from my men.

With a curse, Jared's grip tightened on the phone. "Is everything at the ranch okay?"

"So far, we're status green."

"Keep it that way. I left Courtney and Dylan at my house, but I've got a bigger mess here than I thought. Either the Criswells have gone nuts or someone with a much bigger agenda is trying to burn everything on my land."

"Or, it could be a diversion, Ransom countered. "Do you get the feeling it's as if the guy has a view into exactly what we're doing and thinking?"

Jared spat out a curse. "Exactly. I'm going home."

"We'll keep them safe and I'll contact you if the situation changes," Ransom said. "But that fire needs to be contained before it spreads."

Ransom was right. Jared ended the call and shoved his phone into his pocket. When he slammed open the door a wave of heat hit him. He could hear the horses whinnying from inside the structure.

"Sanderson, take the back. You two—" he pointed to a couple of hands "—work the hoses. The rest of you, get the animals to safety. I want this fire under control before the Carder Fire Department arrives."

The men scurried off. At least he'd had the money to purchase the mobile firefighting unit. Its two hoses would give them a fighting chance of getting this thing under control.

Jared rushed into the building. Brownish-tinged smoke billowed around him, the air thick with soot. He squinted. Roscoe fought one of the quarter horses and pulled him out. "They're spooked bad," he coughed.

Jared grabbed a rag from a bucket and opened the stall to his prized mare. She snorted and reared up. "Easy girl," Jared choked out. Grabbing her bridle, he covered her eyes with the rag and tied it over her ears.

The blindfold calmed her and he led her out, handing her off to one of the hands. "Get them to the east pasture," he shouted.

Jared rushed to the fence when he caught sight of the fire leaping from the roof of the barn to the barracks. Off in the distance the siren of Carder's single fire engine headed their way. It might not be enough.

A shout rang out from inside the vacant winter barracks.

"Stop!" a hoarse voice called out.

"What the hell?" No one was supposed to be staying here. Jared ran to the building and threw open the door. The fire had dropped down from the roof and had created a wall of conflagration. He scanned the ceiling. The timbers would give way soon.

Eyes burning, lungs scorched, he could barely make out the long hallway, but a familiar blue shirt on the ground caught his eye.

"Roscoe!"

Taking a deep breath, he leaped through the fire and hurried to his foreman. A wooden beam lay beside him, and blood trickled from the wound on his forehead. The fire behind them roared. Flames consumed a curtain at one of the windows.

Jared grabbed Roscoe beneath his arms and dragged him to the other end of the building. In just the few seconds since he'd entered the structure, the fire had doubled in size, sweeping across the wood floors as if it were in a conflagration race. The flames licked up the walls, closing in on them.

Above, the wood creaked. Desperate, Jared searched for a means to escape. He tugged Roscoe toward one of the windows, but the fire outran him and suddenly the last opening was barricaded by flame.

"Roscoe? Can you hear me?"

The man's eyes fluttered.

He was still alive.

One wall remained fire-free. For the moment. Slowly sparks soared toward the wood. It would ignite at any moment. Without a sledgehammer or something large and heavy he'd never break through. Spinning around, searching for a way to survive, Jared's gaze penetrated the smoke. He grabbed a chair and ran toward the fire-engulfed window, slammed the wood through, and then raced to pull a blanket from a lower bunk.

He wrapped Roscoe in the blanket, making sure it covered his arms, and shoved his foreman through the opening and dropped him to the ground. Flames licked against the back of the shirt. Heat moved in closer. Jared dove through the opening, twisting in the air to avoid landing on Roscoe, and rolled in the grass. Pricks of heat peppered Jared's back. He yanked the smoking shirt from his body and ground it into the dirt.

They weren't safe yet. Roscoe was too close to the building. He grabbed the man's hands and dragged him away before collapsing backward onto the ground.

Smoke exploded from the opening as oxygen fed the fire. The smoke rose in a plume, darkening the sky. Jared lay there for a moment sucking in air. His eyes burned.

He was alive.

With a groan he sat up and bent over Roscoe. The man's eyes were closed, his jaw slack.

Hand shaking, Jared placed his fingertips on Roscoe's carotid. A faint beat pulsed against him. He tore off the smoke mask and rested his cheek close to the man's mouth. No breath.

"You're not doing this to me, Roscoe. Not today."

He unmasked himself, closed his foreman's nose and puffed a couple of breaths. Then waited.

"Breathe, damn it."

Two more puffs.

Roscoe heaved, Roscoe rolled over, and coughs shuddered through his body. He swiped his mouth. "That's enough. I'm awake, I'm awake," he choked out. "No reason to keep kissin' on me."

Jared sagged, a slight chuckle escaping him. "Don't scare me like that. Breathing isn't optional."

Roscoe wiped his mouth and propped himself up. His eyes widened. "We gotta run."

Jared followed his gaze and let out a loud curse. He grabbed Roscoe by the arm and practically carried him.

The building behind them groaned and shuddered, wood cracking under the heat. The fire roared with intensity sounding like a tornado.

After twenty feet, Jared and Roscoe collapsed on the ground.

Not a moment too soon.

Glass windows exploded; the roof imploded.

Both men turned over and covered their heads.

Debris shot over them, a fire rain bombarding them. When it subsided, Jared stood up and looked around.

Several men were dousing the shrapnel. He bent over. "That was close."

Roscoe looked up at Jared.

"I saw someone. He had a gas can. This was sabotage."

Chapter Eight

The ranch house felt like a prison. Courtney paced back and forth and peered out the small window of the bedroom. She should be *doing* something. Gathering food, water, bandages. Instead, because of the threats, she was stuck here, like the citified woman Roscoe believed her to be.

Plumes of dark brown smoke drifted from the north over the ranch, its acrid scent poisoning the fresh air. An hour ago the sirens of a fire truck and ambulance had screamed across Jared's land.

Still, they waited.

Unaware of the dangers outside, Dylan had discovered energy to spare. He crawled around the room, exploring everything. She'd shut the bathroom door to keep him from getting into trouble. Right now, he'd discovered the closet and a small cubby underneath a short table sitting inside. It was just his size. He threw his stuffed bull out of the closet and crawled to retrieve it before repeating the process a second, third and fourth time.

Courtney would normally have been on the floor enjoying her son, but instead, she recorded every fact she could remember from the time Marilyn had called to warn her. With one eye on him and on Velma, she filled page after page.

The housekeeper sat on the bed holding the gun and staring at the door.

"How much longer do you think?" Courtney asked, her legs bouncing with nerves.

"No telling. Fires are tricky, especially as dry as it's been lately. No news is good news as far as I'm concerned. Nobody tried to get in this room, and Jared hasn't called to evacuate. To me, that's a win."

Dylan crawled between her legs and grabbed on to her pants. He pulled himself up and grinned at her, oh-so-proud of himself for standing alone.

"Look at you, Jelly Bean," she said with a smile. She chucked him under the chin. He hugged her and then scooted beneath the crib, lying on the floor and staring up at its base.

Courtney planted herself cross-legged on the bed. "Jared told me about Alyssa and their daughter."

Velma's eyebrow popped up. "I'm surprised. He doesn't talk about them. Ever."

"I can't believe they never caught the man who killed her."

Velma clicked her teeth together. "That was a bad business. I thought Jared might waste away to nothing. He blamed himself for so long, not being able to save Alyssa from drowning. For months he called out her name in his sleep, promising he'd save her this time."

"She drowned?"

"The murderer pushed her out of the boat at Last Chance Lake and weighed her body down with a tire. Jared did everything humanly possible, but she was under the water too long. He's never forgiven himself."

"I didn't understand how much he must have gone through," Courtney whispered. "And he was never caught. He could still be out there."

"That's Jared's fear. It's why he's built an impenetrable wall around his heart. The truth is, the murderer could easily be dead. He hasn't shown his face since. The ranch has done well. And we haven't had any trouble until the last few months when the Criswells started causing trouble because they want to bleed more money out of Jared."

The sabotage on the ranch couldn't be about Dylan and her. A month ago, she hadn't known Jared's name.

"Jared won't move on, will he?" Courtney twisted her hands in the fabric of her pants.

"He won't take the risk. He can't. Not with anyone. And especially not with his son."

A phone rang and Velma pulled it out of her pocket. "Jared? Is that you?"

She nodded her head and looked over at Courtney giving her a thumbs-up. "We're fine. Barricaded and safe."

She let out a sigh.

"Is he going to be okay?" The worry lines on Velma's brow deepened.

Courtney leaned in and Velma moved the phone so they could both hear.

"Roscoe's sitting in the ambulance now," Jared said. "They're giving him oxygen, but he refuses to go to the hospital."

"Stubborn old coot. Bring him home and I'll make up a room for Derek, too."

Velma ended the call.

"What happened?" Courtney asked.

"Roscoe done and got himself almost killed,

but they put out the fire. Jared's bringing him home. And I'm calling his son." Velma's face held a certain amount of glee. "Derek will give his father hell for not taking care of himself. We may finally convince that boy to come home."

"Finally, we can leave this room."

"Not so fast, honey. Until Jared walks through that door, you and I are staying put."

With a scowl, she returned to her notes, but another half hour didn't provide any insights. A familiar rhythmic knock sounded softly on the door.

Velma grinned and Courtney yanked it open.

"Glad you didn't shoot me through the door, ladies," Jared said.

He looked like he'd been through a war. Soot smeared on his face, his clothes reeked of smoke. Shirt torn and coated with dried blood.

She ran her hands up and down his body, checking for injuries. "Are you hurt?"

Jared quirked a half smile. "You should see the other guy." The smile didn't reach his eyes, though. He shoved his hand through his hair. "I need a shower. I put Roscoe in the old guest room. One of the hands is helping him."

"I'll check on him and make you a dinner that'll stick to your ribs. Both of you," Velma paused and clutched the rifle. "I'm keeping this with me."

"Good idea."

Jared crossed the room and peered underneath the crib, watching Dylan quietly for a few moments. "Slept through it all, did he?"

"He had an adventure but wore himself out a few minutes ago."

Jared picked up the stuffed bull and set it next to his son.

Courtney studied his face. "How bad is the damage?"

"We got lucky. The volunteer fire department and some of my men are staying to finish up. They'll make certain there aren't any live embers to reignite the fire."

"Could they tell what started it?"

"That's a complicated question." Jared rubbed his eye. "A cigarette ignited the burn near the oil derricks, but once the flame reached the barn, someone used an accelerant."

"So it *was* deliberate."

"Not only that, someone hacked into the surveillance cameras' signal." Jared kneaded the back of his neck. "Someone wanted my whole place to burn to the ground."

Cool water sluiced down Jared's back, soothing the heat. He winced as he passed over the scraped skin. He was getting too old to jump through windows. He pressed his hands flat against the shower's tile and bent his head down so the water would do its magic. Roscoe had almost died. He'd almost lost the horses. Several men had been injured. And for what?

They'd disabled the cameras until they could identify the vulnerability. He wanted to scream and shout, "What do you want from me?"

A quick squeeze of shampoo and he lathered up his hair. He had no time for asking questions without answers. He had some decisions to make and actions to take.

He rinsed and turned off the water. After drying, he wrapped a towel around his waist and rubbed his hair as he stepped into the bedroom.

Courtney sat on the king-size bed, waiting for him. Her eyes widened, but she didn't look away.

"You need something?" he asked and pulled a white T-shirt from his drawer then slipped it over his head.

"Sorry. I thought you'd be dressed." She hesitated. "I better go."

"Don't. We need to talk," he said. "Wait here."

He grabbed a pair of briefs and jeans and disappeared into the bathroom. His mind whirling with concern, he slipped them on. When he returned, she sat still, her hands folded in her lap, appearing as proper as a woman could sitting in a man's bedroom.

He didn't quite know how to begin.

"Is Dylan with Velma?" He ran a brush over his wet hair, bringing the short cut to order.

"She's his new favorite person since he discovered her snickerdoodles."

"The way to a man's heart—"

"Is through a sweet tooth in Dylan's case."

Jared tried to smile, but he couldn't. He sat down next to her. "When you arrived on the ranch, you turned my life upside down."

She bowed her head. "I know. I'm sorry."

He lifted her chin with his finger. "I'm not. I'm just sorry I haven't been able to live up to my promise." He let out a long breath. "Whoever's doing this is a step ahead of us. You're not safe here. Every instinct tells me we're sitting in the bull's-eye of a target, and I have no idea who from. If the Criswells are willing to use fire as a weapon, and maybe even hire someone to sabotage security equipment, they're out of control. I can't call the sheriff or Dylan could suffer. If whoever is blackmailing you caused the fire, he's already here. Either way, we have no choice but to act."

"We need another option," she said.

"Unless CTC comes up with a good suspect in the next couple hours, I want us to take you and Dylan into the mountains while they do their job. I probably should have made the move yesterday." He clasped her hands. "I thought I could protect you. I really did."

"You have. We're safe. Dylan's here," she said squeezing his hands in return. "It's not your fault."

"My battle with Ned has compromised your safety. That *is* my fault, but I'm done playing by the rules, because our enemies sure as hell aren't."

"What are you going to do?" she asked.

"See that you're safe, then have a long, serious conversation with Ned so CTC can focus on the man who's threatened you and my son."

A soft knock sounded on Jared's door.

"Come in," he said.

Velma peeked inside. Dylan was balanced on her hip gnawing on a cookie. "Roscoe wants to see you, Jared. And Derek said he could make it here by morning."

"Good. He's the only one I'd trust to keep this place running with Roscoe down. And maybe he can convince his dad to see a doctor."

She frowned. "I wouldn't count on it. He seemed pretty set he's not letting a doctor touch him." Velma looked from him to Courtney and grinned before closing the door softly.

A blush tinged Courtney's cheeks. "I wish there was something I could do," she said softly.

"Maybe there is. Léon left a copy of the files he showed us. They're on my desk. Go through them again. Perhaps you'll see something they missed. I better go see Roscoe."

"Give him my best," she said.

Jared left her and made his way to the old part of the house. Roscoe had refused to get into bed and sat at a makeshift table eating a bowl of soup. He scowled. "That woman's feeding me like I'm an infant," he groused.

"Let her pamper you or she'll make your life a living hell."

"Don't I know it." Roscoe winced when he lifted his arm.

Jared let out a curse. "You need a hospital."

"I need to be here. I saw the guy, Jared. He was wearing a mask, but I saw the triumph in his eyes when he poured the gasoline. He was about five-ten, medium build, brown eyes."

"So not Ned Criswell. Or Chuck. Nobody would call them medium build."

"Maybe one of his hands?"

Jared sat across from Roscoe. "I'm taking Dylan and Courtney into the Guadalupes, up to the old hunting shack. You and I are the only ones who know about it and I can keep them safe."

"You gonna let Ned Criswell destroy this ranch for good?" Roscoe said with a frown.

He lifted his chin, and Jared winced at the scrapes and bruises his foreman sported.

"Look, I'm just going to say it. What if she's making the whole thing up, Jared? What if that woman Marilyn never died. What if this is a big plot to insert herself here and get your money."

"Careful, old man."

"Hear me out. The private investigator could've been mugged. Or she could've hired some thug to kill him. She could have an accomplice who's calling that cell phone. Hell, it could even be a recording. We don't have any proof the threats against that boy are real. Except maybe in her mind. We *do* have proof someone's trying to destroy this ranch. Seems to me you should be worrying about the King legacy and not some elaborate fairy tale spun by a woman you don't know except to take her to bed."

Jared jerked to his feet and grabbed the neck of Roscoe's shirt. "If you hadn't almost died a couple hours ago, I'd slug you for that. Do you think I never considered the possibility? Well, of course I did. The moment she mentioned she needed money for the ransom I suspected her."

A gasp sounded from behind Jared. Courtney stood in the hallway, her face pale. She turned and ran.

"Courtney," he shouted. He glared at Roscoe. "Damn it. If anything happens to them because of this, I don't know if I can forgive you. Ever."

COURTNEY SPED DOWN the hallway, away from Jared. She didn't veer into her bedroom. It was the first place he'd look. Did he really believe she'd planned this whole thing? They didn't know each other well, but she'd trusted him with her son. She'd put her faith in him. His words stabbed at her heart, a betrayal like she'd never experienced.

She made it to his study. This was *his* room. The last place he'd search for her. She walked the room, noticing for the first time the wall of antiques mounted near the stone fireplace. An old horseshoe circa early nineteenth century. A barbed wire wreath. An Apache medicine bundle and an array of Apache knives from different eras. Some with stone blades, some with steel.

Several newer knives were displayed in Jared's gun cabinet. Everyone on this ranch carried a gun of some kind. Courtney had never shot one, but she was tired of depending on others to defend her.

She reached inside and pulled out a sharp knife in a sheath. She slid it from its leather case and the blade glinted in the light.

"You going to gut me with that?" Jared said quietly.

"Maybe." She faced him. "Do you still believe I made this all up to somehow gain control of your money?"

"I considered it."

The words were a slap in the face.

"And dismissed the idea when you responded to the threat to Dylan when Velma left the stuffed bull in his crib. You may be from New York, but you're no actress. Your emotions come through with every expression."

"Roscoe doesn't trust me."

"He's scared. He almost died and he doesn't know how to stop what's happening any more than I do."

"I'm done trying to convince him, Jared."

"You don't have to." Jared took the knife from her. "What's made you so curious about the weapons?"

"I have to be able to defend myself."

"A knife is more difficult to use than a gun,"

he said. "But it can be hidden and used to surprise someone. Try this one. It's a folding knife with a five-inch blade. Legal in Texas. You can slice someone across the belly and run like hell."

She turned it over in her hands and opened and closed it several times.

"If you're going to carry it, stand so you protect your vital organs. Bend your knees and keep your nondominant hand in front of your neck. Your heart and lungs will be harder to reach."

She stood as he instructed. It felt strange. Jared took his position about an arm's length in front of her. "Stand up straight and hold your arm out. See how you can barely reach me."

Nothing she could do at this distance.

"Okay, now go from the other position and slash at my neck or chest. The angle gives you better coverage. The goal isn't to kill me. Just to stop me and get away."

"Let's try it."

He took her through a series of moves at least a dozen times. She bent over and took in several deep breaths. "I don't know if I can do it."

Jared put his hands on her shoulder. "If you're not going to use the weapon, don't carry it. I'll put it away."

She gripped the knife and shoved it into her pocket. "If it's a choice between me and Dylan and someone else, I can use it."

"Have you ever fired a gun?" Jared asked.

She shook her head.

"It's easier to use, but you have to be willing to pull the trigger."

"For Dylan, I'll do whatever it takes."

"Let's go to the root cellar," he said.

Before she could question the bizarre statement, he disappeared out the door and returned with a large target.

"With the cameras hacked, I'm not risking going outside."

He pulled out his Glock and grabbed her hand, leading her downstairs. He set up a back-stop then added several bales of hay. Finally Jared pulled over a small table and placed the gun down on it.

"You ready for this?" he asked.

She took a deep breath and nodded.

"This is a Glock. They don't have a traditional safety that will stop you from pulling the trigger. However, there are internal safeties that will stop it from firing unless you actively pull the trigger. So if you drop it or throw it, it's not going to fire."

He picked up the weapon. "There's an eject button on the side. Flick it and the magazine will come down. That's where the bullets are located."

The magazine fell into his hand and he placed it on the table.

"The other important thing you should know is how to pull the slide back. When you pull the slide back, you can verify there aren't any rounds in the chamber."

He tugged and the Glock clicked open. He gave it to her.

"So, right now, we have an empty, safe weapon."

Jared pulled out a box of bullets. "Load the magazine one bullet at a time." He showed her one. "Now you try."

Seemed easy enough. Courtney pressed a bullet into the magazine and added a second by pressing the first one down and sliding the second one back. Before long she'd filled the magazine.

She could do this. She had to. For Dylan.

"Excellent."

"Push the magazine into the bottom until it clicks."

"It's more simple than I thought."

"Now you pull the slide back. When you do that, you'll have loaded and cocked the gun. It's ready to fire."

Very gently she tugged it back and the weapon clicked in place.

"See how the trigger is now forward. You're ready to shoot. All you have to do is point downrange and pull the trigger."

Courtney squeezed and the gun jerked in her hand. By the time she'd emptied the magazine she had better control. She set the weapon gingerly on the table. "There's quite a bit of kick."

Jared nodded. "Remember, it's not like the movies. Don't plan on shooting farther than ten feet or so. You probably won't hit the target."

"Can I try again?"

"We can practice as much as you want to."

Courtney began loading the Glock again. "I don't want to practice, but I need to. I just hope I don't have to use it," she said.

"If we're faced with life and death, I plan to be there so you don't have to."

Jared stared down at her. "Are we okay?"

She grimaced. "We have to be. Dylan's all that matters." Courtney turned away from him.

Jared opened his mouth to say something but his cell phone interrupted. He tapped the speakerphone. "You have us both, Léon."

"We met with Jamison. Your father is somewhat…indisposed."

"You mean he's drunk. He'd started when I arrived the other day."

"Well, I don't think he's stopped since. He was passed out. We took him to the hospital."

Courtney rubbed her eyes.

"Zane's going through his computers, but he didn't keep great records. His emails are more informative. He was trying desperately to save your family home. Doing anything he could."

"Where do we go from here?" Jared asked.

"I'll send what we have," Léon said. "Can Courtney review the documents? Maybe she'll see inconsistencies we don't."

"Whatever you need," she said.

"Zane will keep searching. There's nothing more I can do here, so I'm heading back. When your father regains consciousness, we can hopefully catch a break." Léon paused. "Ransom informed me about the hack. There are other options, you know. We can make Courtney and her son disappear. We've done it for others."

Jared met Courtney's gaze. She shook her head.

"We're not ready to turn our backs on solving this yet, Léon. But we'll keep it in mind."

Jared hung up the phone. "What do you think? Would you want to change your identity, leave behind everything and start fresh?"

Courtney folded her hands. Could she and Dylan give up everything? "If I thought he couldn't be safe, I'd consider it."

Jared nodded. "Me, too."

"But like you said, I'm not ready to give in to this guy yet." She strode over to his desk. "Can you check your email?"

He smiled at her. "Let's do this."

On a tablet, Courtney reviewed the documents one by one, line by line. She sifted through the notes from CTC and then returned to the documents. Her eyes went blurry.

"There's not enough tying the numbers to a particular person or group," she said. "And nothing that matches the number in the blackmail note."

Courtney retrieved her notepad. She transcribed all the numbers that were smaller than the total. Soon a prick of excitement tingled at the back of her neck.

"Jared. I think I found something. These four numbers add up exactly to $3,680,312.00."

He leaned over and gave her a huge smile. "What do they correspond to?"

"These four entries. I recognize one of the names. It's a Pennsylvania bank."

"Does your family have business in Pennsylvania?"

"I remember my grandmother talking about a mill that had been in the family since the

Industrial Revolution. At one time it was the flagship of the company."

Jared typed the information into a Google search.

"Bingo. A mill owned by your family was shut down without notice five days ago. Several hundred people lost their jobs." Jared picked up his phone. "I'm calling Léon. You may have just solved the mystery."

HIS CAMPOUT WAS well hidden, out of view of the cameras. No one would find him there.

The plethora of computer equipment in the trailer had come in handy. He hadn't expected the challenge of CTC.

They'd been good. They were better than him, but he'd had years to prepare.

He'd faced a few hiccups, but nothing he couldn't handle.

After pressing the jamming signal he searched the smoky remains of the buildings.

No one had died.

Pity.

Unfortunately, the destruction hadn't forced Jared's hand. Yet.

One window of opportunity, that's all that was needed. He scanned the horizon and his gaze lightened on a fresh target.

Yes. That would do. That would do nicely. Jared would never be able to resist.

Chapter Nine

Jared spent the evening in the office with Courtney researching the Pennsylvania textile mill in a small community outside of Allentown. The picture was grim. When Jamison had finally closed the doors, it had decimated the community. There was little left.

There had been numerous protests and they came up with a list of over a hundred suspects, then narrowed it down to those who had been arrested. CTC split the list with them. Unfortunately they'd come up empty.

"This doesn't make sense. Why focus on me and Dylan?" Courtney asked, throwing down the papers in disgust. "It's an awfully convoluted way to make their point. Even if we give them the money, it won't bring the mill back."

"Feels wrong to me, too," Jared said. "Maybe your father has more insight."

Courtney curled up her legs under the sofa. Dylan was safely in bed with the camera monitoring his every breath. She still carried the knife in her pocket and she and Jared had formed a truce of sorts.

Roscoe was another story.

"Until my father sleeps it off," she said, "he won't be able to help us. I've seen him out of it for a couple days."

The picture she painted was one of a very lonely little girl. "How often did it happen?"

"After my mother died, a lot." Courtney shifted on the couch. "He didn't know how to handle her illness, and I didn't make it any easier."

Jared joined her on the sofa.

"Until I was thirteen or so, I didn't know

most dads didn't have that sour smell of alcohol coming off their skin."

Jared stretched his arm across the couch's back, behind Courtney's head. "It must have been hard."

"Not as much as you'd think. My dad had worked all the time anyway. Losing my mom was the hardest thing I ever went through, but our housekeeper made sure I did my homework. I spent weekends with her working for different charities. Cooking at soup kitchens, building homes, that sort of thing."

"Not the childhood I would have guessed," he said.

"What, you thought I went to boarding school and spent all my time shopping?"

He grimaced because she'd absolutely nailed it. That's exactly what he'd thought. He twisted in his seat. "You are a constant surprise and it's very intriguing."

She leaned her head back, resting it on his arm, and turned toward him. "It's funny. I don't think anyone who knows me, knows about that part of my life. Not even my father."

Her words tugged at Jared's heart. She might reside in New York, but the more he learned about her, the more he recognized she didn't *live* there. Not really. Possibilities niggled at the back of his mind; possibilities he shouldn't even consider. But he wanted to.

Courtney shifted in her seat and moved closer to him. "If things were different. If no one was out there trying to hurt us, do you think… I mean, would you…"

She glanced away from him but not before her cheeks reddened. He leaned into her.

"If things were different, nothing would keep me from seducing you in every way I know how until you never wanted to leave."

The words left his lips before he could stop them.

Her eyes dilated and she eased closer. "I'd like to pretend. Just for tonight."

Jared's body tensed and he stilled. "The future—"

She pressed her finger to his lips. "The future is tomorrow. We were interrupted once. I want tonight. I want all of you tonight, Jared."

He saw no hesitation in her eyes, just like that night a year and a half ago, but this time their senses weren't dulled by tequila. He tugged her into his lap and wrapped his arms around her. She turned to face him and cupped his cheeks in her hands.

She brought her mouth down to his and unleashed the passion. She straddled his hips and ground her pelvis against him. His body hardened under her.

Jared thrust his hands into her short, silky hair and pressed open her lips. His tongue dueled with hers in an age-old ritual. Unlike the last time, he knew exactly where she longed to be touched.

He nibbled at the base of her jaw and let his hands slip to the sides of her blouse down to her hips and tugged the material from her waist. In one easy movement he removed her shirt and lowered his mouth to the curve of her breast. She arched against him and her soft groan urged him onward.

Soon she was nude from the waist up and he feasted on her curves, evoking shivers of ecstasy from her.

Her hands clutched at his T-shirt and she pushed it over his head, her hands exploring the muscles of his chest. She pressed him back against the sofa and he let her touch him, her gentle fingers outlining the scrapes and burns from the fire. He didn't feel anything but pleasure, though.

His body hardened under her and when he couldn't bear it any longer he lifted her up and stood.

He could hear his labored breathing and hers. She explored his skin and slipped her fingers beneath the waist of his jeans. She flicked open the button and lowered his zipper, but he stilled her hands.

"Not so fast," he whispered. "You're over-dressed."

In no time, he'd removed the remainder of her clothes and she stood before him. Her body had changed since having Dylan. If anything, she was more beautiful than ever. He shirked his jeans and pulled her back into his arms, lowering her to the rug on the floor.

She tugged him closer, then shifted her weight with a laugh, reversing their positions. She propped herself up on his chest and smiled down at him.

"I like pretending."

"So do I." He flipped her over and urged her legs apart. Once he'd slipped on a condom he paused, looking deep into her eyes.

"You're certain."

"Very."

Whereas before their movements had been frantic and heated, Jared didn't want their love-making to end. Slowly, tenderly, he pressed inside her until he was buried deep. His head dropped onto her shoulder and he sighed.

He was home.

A STRONG ARM rested on Courtney's bare skin. For a moment, she couldn't quite figure out where she was. Morning sun spilled through the curtains in Jared's study.

She lay cocooned in his arms, covered by a soft quilt.

Last night she'd told him they could pretend. She'd lied. She didn't want to pretend. She wanted last night to go on and on. She wanted every kiss, every touch to be real, but she knew she could never convince Jared. And how could she argue? She'd do anything to keep her family safe. Even at the expense of her own happiness. Or her own life.

As would he.

He'd proven it, and it was one of the reasons she…she loved him.

Oh God. She loved him.

Her chest tightened. She could hardly breathe as the truth settled over her heart. But she couldn't doubt her feelings. She shared parts of herself with him no one else knew. He'd gifted her with his own heartbreaking past.

She'd give anything to be able to heal him, to make the hurt go away. She cuddled down deeper against him.

Jared tightened his arms around her.

"Good morning," he whispered, kissing her hair. He let his fingertip travel down her arms and she shivered at his touch.

A loud cowbell rang outside. He let out a low curse. "Breakfast for the men. It must be six."

Courtney glanced at the phone Jared had laid beside their makeshift bed last night. Dylan had started squirming a bit. He'd make his presence known soon.

She sat up and searched for her clothes. They were strewn near the sofa.

"We probably can't make it to our bedroom without someone seeing us."

"We can try," she said.

Jared grabbed his jeans and tossed her clothes to her. Quickly they dressed and Jared stuck his head out the door.

"Clear," he said and led her into the hallway.

They rushed toward their bedrooms just as Velma appeared from the kitchen. She took one look at them, grinned widely and turned back the way she'd come.

"So much for sneaking around."

A loud pounding sounded on the front door.

"I'll get it," Jared said, tucking his shirt into his pants.

Courtney hovered out of sight. Maybe CTC had uncovered something.

Jared opened the door to a blond-headed man wearing an expensive suit and a wide grin.

"J.K.!" he shouted.

"Derek." Jared grinned and embraced the man. He shut the door and locked the dead bolt. "I'm glad you're here. Roscoe will be thrilled. And surprised."

So, this was Roscoe's son and Jared's childhood friend. She'd never seen such a welcome on his face.

Derek's gaze paused on her. He smiled at Jared. "Have you got something to tell me?"

Jared followed his line of sight. For a moment he paused. Courtney froze. Maybe he didn't want her to meet his friend. Maybe—

"This is the mother of my son," Jared said, holding out his hand to her.

Hesitantly, she made her way over to him and took her hand. He entwined his fingers with hers.

"Your what?" Derek's expression turned from a smile to shock.

Courtney held out her hand. "I'm glad to meet you."

Derek grinned and pulled her in for a tight hug. "Anyone who got this guy to return to the land of the living deserves more than a handshake."

She smiled at him.

"You done good, J.K. I can tell she's a class act."

Courtney tucked her hair behind her ear. He was more like Velma than Roscoe, that was for sure.

Derek crossed his arms in front of him. "I should've come back sooner. "Dad's been emailing me and he didn't say a thing about you two. Of course he didn't say a word about the fire either."

Courtney met Jared's gaze before he responded to his friend "It's one of the reasons I'm glad you're here."

At Jared's solemn tone, Derek stilled. "The same reason you're wearing a Glock?"

In a clipped tone, Jared brought his best friend quickly up to date on everything. Derek whistled under his breath. "And the fire?"

"May be related to Courtney. Maybe to the

Criswells. We just don't know and I need another set of eyes to keep everyone safe. Someone who knows this land like I do."

Derek glanced down at the floor, avoiding Jared's gaze. "I haven't lived here for a long time, J.K. I'm not sure I'm the best choice."

"That's bull. You care about this place as much as I do. You always have."

For several moments Derek didn't speak. Jared waited. Courtney could only hope his friend agreed. They needed all the help they could get.

The furrow cleared from Derek's brow. "You've got me. I'll do whatever I can. Now, how's Dad doing? Really."

Jared squeezed her hand tight and a light settled in his eyes. Courtney leaned into him. Piece by piece things were looking up.

"Roscoe's about like you'd expect," Jared led them into the study. "Stubborn, but improving. He's staying in the old wing of the house while he's recuperating so Velma can keep an eye on him."

Derek grinned. "I'm sure he likes that. A lot."

"Please." Jared shuddered. "Just don't go there. I pretend I don't know what's going on between them, and I like it that way."

The expression on Derek's face slipped a bit. "First I need to see Dad, then put me to work."

Jared slapped Derek on the back. "You bet. Go visit, and then we'll figure it out. Man, I'm glad you're here."

Derek grinned at his friend. "Me, too. It's been much too long."

AFTER A QUICK SHOWER—which he would have much rather shared with Courtney—Jared exited his room with a new attitude. Maybe their luck was changing. Derek had come home to help out. They'd discovered a connection between Courtney's father and the money.

The only problem with that was Courtney and Dylan would leave soon, and Jared would miss them. More than he could have imagined.

He walked into the kitchen and poured a cup of coffee.

Velma grinned. "Derek the wanderer is back."

"He certainly is."

"Did I hear my name taken in vain?" Derek asked.

Velma raced over to him and hugged him close. "Roscoe's missed you. You need to come home more."

"Business has me hopping," Derek said. He turned to Jared. "I'm heading to my room and get a shower and change out of my work digs into jeans and boots. Burberry and barns don't mix."

"I'd agree with you there. Not to mention those shoes. Italian?"

Derek nodded. "I checked in on Dad. He's resting, so for now I'll check in with Frank about where he wants me to stand guard. See you later?"

Jared nodded. "Hey, Derek. Thank you. It means a lot that you're here."

"I wouldn't be anywhere else."

Derek disappeared into the old part of the house, and Jared scooped up an egg sandwich from the tray Velma had stacked on the sideboard. He sat down at the table and munched on his breakfast. Velma eyed him for several minutes before finally sitting across from him.

She grinned with that knowing, scary expression that had terrified him from the time he'd gone through puberty.

"What do you want to know that I'm not going to tell you?" he asked between bites.

"I can't believe he came home. His father's been trying to tempt him for two years. I didn't think I'd succeeded."

Jared eyed the coffee cake across the room. He rose and fetched the plate before returning to his seat. He took a large bite of the cinnamon and sugar treat and followed it with a large swallow of coffee. He nearly rolled his eyes in pleasure.

With a shrug he took another bite. "I texted him after you called and let him know I needed him to convince Roscoe to the doc for a full physical."

Velma frowned at that. "The cough?"

Jared nodded. This time his cake tasted almost like sawdust. "It doesn't sound good."

"I know. I've been worried, too. Whatever the reason, I'm glad he's here."

"Can you believe he jumped right in to help with the guard duty. With Tim injured, we could use all the help we can get."

Velma folded a napkin and took a deep breath. "Which brings me to another topic of conversation."

Jared flushed. "If it's about this morning—"

"I'm not a prude, boyo, but I am worried about you. And about Courtney and Dylan.

Are you going to ask them to stay after this is all over?"

Jared stared down at his cup. "I wish I could, but it's not possible."

Velma shot to her feet. "I think what you're doing is wrong. That little boy needs a daddy. Courtney needs a partner. And you, Jared, need someone who loves you more than anything in the world. Don't let that SOB who stole your family five years ago win again."

Velma's eyes went wide in shock and she spun away from him. She headed toward the laundry room and slammed the door.

Courtney walked in and let out a low whistle. "I think you're in trouble."

Jared flushed. "I'm sorry you had to hear that. She doesn't understand."

Courtney stole a small piece of coffee cake from his plate and popped it in her mouth. "She understands perfectly. She doesn't want you to live your life in fear."

"I explained to you what happened. I can't

risk your life or Dylan's, not when the person who hates me is so willing to kill those closest to me.

One sharp push and Courtney shoved her chair back. "I understand, Jared. And maybe once we've caught the blackmailer I'll feel differently, but right now, I need you by my side, and I'm getting used to it. The truth is, I'm not so sure I want to give you up when this is over."

She stalked out of the kitchen. Jared watched the sway of her hips as she turned the corner to head back to her bedroom. Was he a fool for paying attention to the past?

A sudden wave of shouts hit just outside. Jared shot to his feet and raced to the front door. He met Tim coming up the stairs.

"What's wrong?" Jared asked. Tim's recent cast had already taken on a shade of Texas dirt.

"Frank and I were doing rounds on the west pasture. We found a slew of dead cattle and even more with tremors and convulsions. I've never seen anything like it."

Jared's face turned to stone except for the pulsing at his jaw. Tim took a step back and Jared forced himself to calm down.

"What caused it?"

Jared had a bad feeling he knew exactly what the culprit was.

An older cowboy pushed in. "Someone salted the water."

The worst thing you could do to animals. And it wouldn't only affect the cattle.

"What's the damage?" Jared asked.

Tim shook his head. "No telling how many we lost. Or how many wild animals were poisoned. We blocked the watering hole but ever since Old Man Criswell dammed up the water, fresh is hard to come by. The cows were a bit dehydrated anyway, and that salt did them in."

Jared paced back and forth. Was this Criswell again? It had to be. Why would a blackmailer from Pennsylvania want to poison cattle in Texas? It didn't make any sense.

Jared faced Tim. "Take care of the carcasses," he ordered. "We'll need samples to send off to the lab to prove the cause. And I want you to keep an eye out for tire tracks, human tracks, bottles, anything that could point to the person who poisoned the water."

"I saw tire tracks. Like the ones behind the barn where the shot was fired. Same tread."

Jared rubbed his chin. "Really? We thought it might be a large truck. Like an F-350, didn't we?"

Tim nodded.

Jared slammed his hat against his jeans. "You know what, Criswell has gone too far this time. I don't know if it's Ned or Chuck or both, but I've had it." He turned to Tim and Frank. "What are you two waiting for? Get back out there."

The two men hurried away and Jared glanced

over his shoulder. Derek stood near the house and Courtney stood in the foyer of his house.

He strode over to them. "Derek, keep watch here. I'm heading over to the Criswell ranch. I shouldn't be more than an hour or so. This feud has gone on long enough. Besides if they don't stop meddling, we'll never be able to narrow our investigation long enough to catch the blackmailer."

She grasped his arm. "Be careful. Please. I have a bad feeling about your leaving."

"Don't worry about me."

"Of course I'll worry." she said. "You're a stubborn man who doesn't have the sense to grab on to what you have, but I must admit I'm fond of you anyway."

"Fond?" Jared rested his lips against her cheek.

"That's all you get until you're back safe and sound."

Jared cupped her cheek. "I'll have my phone

and radio with me. If you hear anything from CTC or the blackmailer, call immediately."

"That's what terrifies me, Jared. Why haven't we heard?"

HE PUT DOWN his binoculars and smiled. Jared's beat-up pickup had left the property. Everything was going according to plan. Well, maybe not everything. There'd been more collateral damage than he'd wanted, but in the end, his victory would be worth it.

Jared had no idea what was in store for him. He might have clawed his way back the last time, but this time...this time he'd understand everything.

He opened the back of his SUV. The supplies had been easy enough to steal.

Before night fell, it would be over. The Last Chance Ranch would have no more chances.

Chapter Ten

Courtney watched Jared drive toward the north, her heart filled with trepidation. The guards acknowledged her one by one. She wasn't alone, even if it felt like it. She'd become used to having him around.

Probably not a good thing.

She went back into the house and into the kitchen. Velma had jerry-rigged a high chair for Dylan and she was tempting him with cereal.

"Everything okay?"

"The little one and I are doing fine." Velma glanced over at her. "How are you?"

"I've never seen Jared so angry," Courtney said. "You don't think he'll go too far with the Criswells, do you?"

"I couldn't say. Especially if they killed his cattle and he can prove it."

Courtney sat next to her son and tried to tempt him with some melon. "Velma, who on the ranch knows the most about watering cattle?"

The housekeeper turned away from the stove with an inquiring expression. "Roscoe. Why do you ask?"

"No reason." Other than it had become clear over the last couple of days that whoever had sabotaged the ranch was one step ahead of them. "Could you watch Dylan for me? I think Roscoe and I need to clear the air."

Courtney kissed Dylan on the forehead and headed to the old part of the house. She entered the hallway where the nursery was located. She didn't really know which room was Roscoe's.

Slowly she walked down the hallway. She passed the old nursery door. She knocked on a closed door very lightly.

No answer. Gingerly she cracked it open. Empty and abandoned.

She made her way to the next one and rapped on it.

"I told you I'm not hungry, Velma."

Something clattered inside and a loud curse echoed through the door. Courtney pushed inside and gasped.

Roscoe lay on the floor, his body bandaged, bruised and battered, the contents of a breakfast tray strewn all around the room.

When he recognized her he flushed. "What do you want?"

"Do you need some help?"

He braced himself on the bed and rose to his feet. "I can handle it."

"Everyone needs help now and then."

Pretending to be calmer than she was, Courtney knelt down and scraped the ruined toast, sausage and eggs back on the tray. Luckily the carafe of coffee was sealed.

"The coffee looks to be intact," she said. "Would you like a cup?"

Roscoe scowled and slid back into bed. "Doc said 'no' with the medication he gave me."

Courtney winced. "Ouch."

The foreman raised a brow. "You an addict, too?"

"I'm not human until my fourth cup, usually. I had to cut back when I found out I was pregnant."

"How hard was it?"

"The first few weeks weren't pretty. Between morning sickness and caffeine headaches no one wanted to be around me."

Roscoe chuckled. "When Velma learns I'm off coffee and decaf is little more than hot colored water so she's going to force tea down my throat. I hate stuff that tastes like watery weeds worse."

Courtney stared at the wiry old man and

laughed. "Hard to argue with that." She placed the tray on the too small nightstand. "Why don't you like me?"

"I don't know you," He frowned. "But Jared changed the minute you stepped out of the silly car you rented. That's not good for the ranch." He cleared his throat. "But I was wrong. Jared set me straight about a few things. And Velma told me that boy of yours is a pistol just like young Jared."

"Did you know him when he was a baby?"

"Nah. My son and I moved to the ranch when he and Jared were boys. After my wife passed from leukemia."

"I'm sorry. My mom died of a brain cancer."

"You know how it is, then. Derek took it hard. She understood him. My boy's too smart for his own good, that's for sure."

Roscoe stretched out a shaky hand. "Truce?" he asked.

"How about we just start over?"

"Deal. Why did you come see me after the

things I said about you? I thought you'd avoid me at all costs."

"I probably would have except for what happened to the cattle last night."

"What's going on?"

Roscoe straightened up tall in bed.

Now Courtney wondered if she hadn't made a big mistake. Too late now. She told him about the salt in the water.

Roscoe's face turned alarmingly red and a flurry of curses exploded from his lips. "I wouldn't have thought Ned Criswell would go that far."

"Jared's going to see him and have it out. I'm worried."

"He go alone?"

She nodded.

"Damn it. That isn't good. Ned Criswell's a mean SOB, but he's a good rancher and he values water and the livestock. His son, on the other hand, has no honor. Ned might have ordered his guys to dig up the posts so the cattle could escape and stampede, but if I had to bet, I'd say Chuck salted the water."

"Why would he do such a thing?"

"Because he hates ranching and he knows if his dad can convince Jared to pay them off, he's set for life. He hates living in Carder, and he'd love for his old man to keel over so he can take the money and head to the big city. You aren't gonna live in or around Carder if you can't tolerate the main business in the community. Everyone in the area except those CTC guys make a living off the land or off those who work the land." Roscoe picked up his phone. "I'll get Sheriff Redmond to go out and check on them."

Courtney grabbed the phone from his hand. "You can't."

"What the hell's wrong with you?"

"The man who threatened Dylan said if I contacted the police, they'd hurt him."

Roscoe leaned back against his pillow. "So

that's why Jared called off the sheriff. Why didn't he just say something?"

"He was trying to protect you, I guess."

"The boy's lost a lot in his life. He's always trying to protect everyone." Roscoe put out his hand. "Give me that phone."

She hesitated to place it in his hand.

"I'm sending Derek to the Criswells to watch Jared's back. Jared won't jump down his throat. Hell, I'd go if I could, but even I'm not stupid enough to try to drive all the way out there like this."

"Jared wanted Derek to stay here, to watch us."

"We've got plenty of guards," Roscoe frowned." And my boy will keep Jared safe."

"Thanks, Roscoe." Courtney kissed his grizzled cheek. The tension in her shoulders had eased a bit knowing Jared had backup. "I'm glad we aren't enemies, anymore."

"Go on, get out of here. I'm afraid once

things get back to normal, I'm going to fall for you just like Jared and Velma have."

Courtney smiled at him. "That's the way I like it."

THE SMELL OF bacon drifted through the house. Courtney carried the empty breakfast tray back to Velma. "Roscoe and I aren't at war anymore."

The housekeeper turned to her with a huge smile. "I knew he'd grow on you."

Velma lifted the bacon from the skillet and rested it on paper towels. Courtney peered at the scrumptious-looking meat. She couldn't resist and snagged a piece.

"How's Dylan?" She munched on the treat.

Velma placed another half-dozen strips in the pan and the crackling of frying and the delicious scent filled the room. "Oh, the boyo has sure taken to that little blue bull considering all the trouble the animal caused."

Courtney knelt down and kissed her son's

head. "Are you having a good time with Miss Velma, Jelly Bean."

Her son tugged the blue bull and babbled at it.

"I wish I knew kid talk. No doubt he and that bull have had some very interesting conversations."

Velma's eyes crinkled at the corners. "He's a good boy, Courtney. You've done a wonderful job with him. Such a good disposition."

"I got lucky."

"Don't kid yourself, sweetie. In spite of being on your own, that baby's not nervous around strangers. He's lovely and happy. That doesn't come from luck. It comes from his mama's confidence and love."

"Thanks, Velma. That means a lot."

Courtney kissed Dylan's nose. Most of the time when she looked at him she saw Jared, but his dimples, they belonged to her father.

"Velma, do you think you could watch him for a while longer?"

"I thought you'd never ask."

"I'll be in the study talking to my father. Hopefully he's feeling better."

"Don't you worry about a thing." The housekeeper waved Courtney away.

Leaving her son in good hands, she pushed open the mahogany doors and entered Jared's study.

They'd left the room in chaos this morning. The quilts they'd slept on were still strewn on the floor. Courtney folded them and placed them on the couch, grabbed the CTC folders and rounded the desk.

If they were ever going to catch this guy, they needed a break, and her father was the only one who might be able to help.

Sinking in the suppleness of Jared's leather chair, she picked up the cell phone he'd loaned her. She dialed her father's number. One ring, two rings. Four rings. No answer. She debated whether to leave a message when a voice filtered through the earpiece.

"H…h…hello?"

Slurred but coherent.

"Father?"

"Courtney? Courtney, what's going on? These men grabbed me from my hotel and forced me into a hospital. I'm lucky they didn't confiscate my phone."

How long had it been since she'd heard him in such a state? Years. "Father, do you remember me coming to visit?"

The phone went silent.

If he'd blacked out, he really may not be able to help them. Then what would they do?

She forced her voice to stay calm. "I visited you a couple days ago. Remember. I brought Dylan. It was the day you had to leave the house."

He let out a harsh laugh. "You mean the day they stole our things and kicked me out of our home? The day they took the paintings, the furniture, the china, the crystal. Everything."

Courtney winced. He wasn't doing well at

all. "That's. I need to ask a few questions, and I need you to try hard to remember."

"You can say it, Courtney. You need me to not screw up again. Like the day I failed you and Dylan. I didn't have any money." He let out a low sob. "And I drank the entire bottle of Cognac. I blacked out."

"Are you feeling better now? Are they taking good care of you?"

"I'll survive. We've been here before, haven't we?" He coughed and it turned into a fit. Just hearing the congestion in his lungs reignited the worry. "Of course life will be different. I'll have to find a job when I get out of here."

"How about you take things one day at a time for now?" Courtney spoke slowly and patiently, but inside she wanted to grab hold of him and get answers. She composed herself and tried to refocus him. "Father, I need your help. Can you concentrate for me? It's very important." She leaned forward in Jared's leather chair, her pen poised on her notebook.

"Those men have been picking my brain since they woke me up," he groused. "I don't know about any three million dollars and change. Except I wish I had it."

"Father, I need information concerning the loans you took out for the mill in Pennsylvania. They add up to over three million dollars. It's a very specific amount of money."

Her father laughed out load. "Well, of course it is. I split the loans up so I'd be able to keep the mill going and have a little flexibility. Lot of good that did."

"That's it? No, there had to be more to the blackmail note. It was personal. They'd threatened her son.

"Was there anyone who caused a lot of trouble while you were working on getting the loans for the mill?"

He laughed. "Of course not. It kept the mill afloat, but out of the blue last week the bank called them all in. I couldn't pay. Had to close the mill. End of story."

She rubbed her temple. "Who would have been the most upset? The workers? The town? Local politicians?"

"All of the above."

Courtney stared at the sheet of paper and sank back into the desk chair. Her father rambled off a few more random details, like an interview he gave to the local town paper, but they didn't seem relevant. The number in the ransom note represented the loss of the mill, but they'd punished her father already. Who would gain by threatening to kill her son? Did they simply want the money?

This felt wrong.

Maybe Jared would see an angle she didn't. She dialed his number and he picked up right away.

"Are you okay?" he asked, his voice crackling.

"This is a terrible connection." she said.

"I'm heading into a valley. I might lose you for a couple of minutes."

Sure enough, his voice dropped off.

She dialed again, but he didn't answer. She redialed several times then waited a few minutes. When she picked up the phone again, several strange hits of static sounded, then no signal. That was odd. It had never happened before at the ranch.

Courtney stilled. She perked her ears to listen carefully. She could hear discussions and laughter outside. Nothing worrisome. And yet, a tingling took up residence at the back of her neck, a foreboding that tasted sour at the back of her throat. She rose from behind the desk and strode across the study, checking her phone in different parts of the room. Still, no service.

She made her way to the mahogany doors. Instead of hurrying through, though, she eased them open. She peered into the foyer.

It was deserted. And silent. Everything looked normal.

Then her gaze landed on the front door dead bolt. It was unlocked.

Against Jared's rules.

Her throat closed off. Her gaze darted behind her to the gun rack.

She backed up.

"Oh no, you don't," a voice whispered from just behind the door.

The strangely quiet tone he used to speak made it impossible to identify his voice. Maybe that was the point.

Courtney whirled around, but a man in a ski mask grabbed her by the arm and shoved her against the wall just inside the study and closed the door behind them. He pressed his forearm against her throat. "I decided not to call," he whispered. "This time, I came in person."

She froze. It was *him*. She had no doubt, but she couldn't figure out how he'd managed to sneak through the security. How was it possible?

"Are you going to behave or cause trouble?" he whispered. "If you're good, I may let your son live. If not, I have no trouble killing him as soon as I see him."

He pressed harder against her windpipe. Spots circled in front of her eyes.

"P-please," she gasped.

He released his grip slightly.

"I—I'll do whatever you want."

If she could only delay enough, maybe Velma would escape with her son. Maybe Jared would get there and save them all. He wasn't that far away.

"I thought you might," he whispered. "You haven't figured out the game yet, though. None of you have." He chuckled, a satisfied arrogant laugh that burned fury in Courtney's skin.

"Hold your hands in front," he said softly. He bound them, cinching the knot tight.

He paused, his brown eyes narrowed. "If you don't follow all of my instructions," he whispered, "I will kill everyone in this house, including your son. Just like I killed your babysitter in that penthouse."

If she'd had any doubts this was the man they were looking for, she didn't anymore.

He opened the study door and stood at her back, his body touching hers. She shuddered. He bent toward her ear. The knit mask brushed against her cheek. "Don't speak, don't cry out. Walk where I guide you in complete silence. Do you understand?"

"Yes."

He slapped her face. Hard. Her head whipped to the side. "I told you, no talking. Just nod your head. Do you understand?"

She nodded.

"Excellent."

His perpetual whisper creeped her out each time he spoke. It was as if he were less than human. He pushed her through the study door and down the hall to the guest room where she'd been staying. She said nothing. She couldn't risk Dylan's life. Or anyone else's.

"You've never been helpless a day in your life, have you? Well, you're going to find out exactly what it's like to feel that way."

She tried to move her arms and get at the knife in her pocket, but when she adjusted her shoulders, he slapped her again.

"Don't play games, Courtney. I can see your moves coming a mile away."

He shoved her into the bedroom and kicked the door closed. There had to be a way to warn Velma. The cameras were no help. The app was on Jared's phone.

Unless he looked at it. A small sprig of hope ignited until her captor pushed her face down onto the bed.

"Turn over."

Oh God. What was he going to do? She had no choice. She complied.

"Stay there. And remember what I said. If you move, they are all dead."

He gripped her throat, and she could tell without a doubt, he could snap her neck if he so chose. He loomed above her. "Will you obey me?"

She nodded.

"Don't worry, Courtney," he said with a slight smile. "I'll be back soon."

He left her lying there. She stood up and scanned the room. Her eyes fell on a picture. If she broke the glass she could use it to break free. When he came back, she could stop him, as long as he didn't have Dylan with him.

She grabbed the photo frame. How much noise would it make if she slammed it against the bathtub?

Before she could decide a loud crash clattered from somewhere near the kitchen. Velma shouted in terror. "You're not taking that baby," she screamed.

Dylan squealed in terrified cries. Panicked, Courtney ran to the bathroom and threw down the frame.

The noise was drowned out by a horrific crash. Then a loud thud.

A gunshot rang out.

God no.

Footsteps raced across the floor.

"Courtney! Jared!" Léon's voice shouted.

"I'm here!" Courtney replied.

After what seemed forever, he opened the door. He held Dylan in his arms.

He whipped out a knife and cut through the rope.

She reached out for Dylan and pressed him against her breast, patting his back to calm down her terrified baby. "Shh. Jelly Bean. Mama's here. You're safe. I promise."

"When did you get back?"

"Just arrived. Lucky thing. You okay for a minute?" Léon asked.

"Did you get him?" Courtney asked. "Please say you killed him."

Léon shook his head with a scowl. "He got away. I'm not sure how, but he's gone."

Her head fell on top of Dylan's. "Then it's not over."

Léon shook his head. "Take care of your son. I have to help Velma. She hit her head pretty badly protecting Dylan."

Courtney followed him to the kitchen. She gasped in dismay. Velma lay on the floor in the midst of shattered glasses and dishes. Blood oozed from a head wound. Her eyes were shut, her skin pale.

Courtney knelt down beside her. Léon felt for a pulse.

"She's alive, but we need to get her to a hospital as soon as possible. Where's Jared?"

"Driving back from the Criswell ranch, I hope. I tried calling but there was no service."

"Jared has his own tower. He rarely loses service."

"*He* did it."

"That's my guess."

Léon rose and wet a rag to clean some of the blood away from Velma's injury. "She was hit hard."

He glanced over his shoulder. "Keep trying

the phone. We need to warn Jared to keep an eye out for someone suspicious on the ranch."

Courtney hit the redial button. Over, and over, and over again.

Finally she had four bars.

Jared answered. "What the hell happened? I've been trying to reach you for a half hour."

She could hardly speak. "He was here, Jared. He broke in and tried to take Dylan."

Chapter Eleven

Jared pressed the accelerator to the floor. The beat-up truck bounced over the dirt roads. He wiped away the blood at the corner of his mouth. Thank God for Derek, Courtney, and Velma. Dylan was safe, but damn it, Jared should have been there to protect his family.

His family. He'd come to think of them that way in just a few short days. He slammed his hand on the steering wheel. "Come on. Faster."

He glanced in the rearview mirror. He looked like hell. Ned could throw a few good licks for a man old enough to be Jared's father. Chuck had cowered. He'd also admitted to sabotaging the fence posts, stealing the pin on Angel Maker's gate and flicking the cigarette near the oil wells. He'd denied firing the shot, dousing the stalls with gasoline and salting the water, though.

For some reason, Jared believed him.

Chuck would pay for what he'd done. The man was just lucky no one had died.

But his denial begged the question, was Courtney's blackmailer also responsible for the destruction on Jared's land? Or was there someone else still out there?

One thing at a time.

He drove onto his land and closed in on the ranch house as fast as the truck would allow. He didn't hesitate when he reached the perimeter alarm system. The sirens sounded and his men scrambled, their weapons at the ready.

Jared slammed on the brakes and the tires skidded in the dirt in front of the house. Courtney met him at the door, Dylan in her arms. She ran to him and he hugged them close.

"Are you okay?" He pulled back and studied her face. He touched her cheek lightly. "He hit you?"

"I'm fine. He threatened to kill everyone in the house if I didn't obey him." Her face went pale. "I didn't know what to do, so I followed his instructions."

Jared placed his hands on her arms. "You did the right thing. There are times to fight, and situations where it's best to bide your time. We know he's killed before. You and Dylan are alive and safe."

Jared kissed her forehead, so as not to hurt her bruised face. "How's Velma?"

"She hasn't regained consciousness. Tim took her to the hospital and Roscoe went with him," Courtney said. "She wouldn't let him have the baby. She and Léon saved Dylan from that man."

"Where's Derek?" Jared could feel the fury rising in his chest. Had his friend let him down? "He was supposed to watch you."

"He went to help you. We thought we were safe."

"He never showed." Jared's gut sank. "We have to find him." His gaze snapped to Courtney. "Is there any clue as to his identity?"

"He wore a ski mask and he whispered. All I can tell you is that his eyes are brown."

"So, we're no closer to identifying him, and now Derek's missing." Jared ran his hands over Courtney to make certain she was all right. "This wasn't supposed to happen." Jared turned to Léon. "No more games. No more trying to draw this guy out until we have actionable intel. I want Courtney and Dylan out of here. Now."

The operative winced and nodded in agreement. "Ransom has his plane gassed and waiting for you at the airport. We're not filing a flight plan or revealing the destination to anyone until you're in the air." He scanned the area surrounding them, his gaze piercing.

"Come inside. No telling when or if the guy will come back."

Holding Courtney close to his side, they walked in the house.

"You're taking my truck. There's no way to track in, even for a hacker. You'll leave the kidnapper's phone here. When you leave, you'll keep your hat pulled low and your face down," Léon said. "I want it to appear as if you're still here."

"What about me and the baby?" Courtney asked.

"I have an equipment box that you'll fit in. Jared can carry Dylan in a duffel and we'll stow the car seat in a garbage bag. You'll all go into the back end of the SUV until you arrive at the airport. The perp will expect us to be hunkering down for a while. Hopefully long enough for you to get away.

Jared nodded. "I like the idea."

"Then let's do it."

A half hour later, Jared started Léon's SUV

and pulled down the road leaving Last Chance Ranch. The tinted windows hid the luggage area from view.

The vehicle rumbled over a cattle guard. The rough ride shook the SUV waking Dylan. The baby let out a cry that made Jared wince.

"Just a minute, little guy. Mama will get you soon. I promise."

Jared's voice calmed Dylan a bit, but it didn't last long.

Once they were off his property, Jared called out to Courtney. "Clear."

She pushed open the metal case. Dylan lifted his arms. "Ma."

"Stay hunkered down," Jared said. "We can't take any chances."

"I will." Courtney pulled Dylan into her arms and cuddled him. Jared kept his eyes on the road. The small airport got very little traffic. They shouldn't run into anyone.

They reached the outskirts of Carder. The ribbon of asphalt cut through the landscape.

A bright blue sky met the horizon. It would be good flying weather.

Jared reached a dip in the road and a white vehicle drove toward them. His hands clenched on the steering wheel.

"Car coming. Keep low."

The sheriff's lights took shape on top of the SUV the closer they got. Blake Redmond would recognize one of CTC's vehicles. It shouldn't be a problem.

Jared whizzed by the sheriff. Almost there.

A squeal of tires came from behind him and a siren started screaming.

"What's wrong?" Courtney asked.

"Nothing. I'll pull over and get rid of Blake. If I was speeding he can write me a ticket."

Jared pulled the vehicle over. The sheriff's car stopped behind him. Blake rounded the car and Jared rolled down the window.

"Look, Blake—"

The sheriff whipped off his sunglasses. "Where do you think you're going, Jared?"

"Since when do you go all official on me?"

"Don't go there." Blake shook his head. "I gotta ask. Do you have a gun in the vehicle?"

"Of course. I'm wearing it. I have a conceal carry permit."

"Nine millimeter, right? According to your permit."

"Yes." Jared didn't like the wincing expression on the sheriff's face. "What's going on, Blake?"

"I need you to step out of the vehicle."

He glanced behind him and met Courtney's frightened gaze. He gave her a quick nod. If he could keep her hidden, even from a friend, that was one less person who knew where they were. "Look, Blake. Whatever it is has to wait. I've got a plane—"

"I'm sorry, Jared. You're not going anywhere. Not until we straighten a few things out."

"I have no idea what you're talking about."

"You got a nice-sized bruise on your chin,

and that eye's not looking so good. You get into a fight?"

Jared didn't like where this was headed. "So what if I did? Since when's that a crime."

"My information says you took a drive out to Ned Criswell's house? Is that true?"

From Blake's expression, Jared had the distinct impression the sheriff wanted him to deny the allegation. Trouble was he couldn't.

"Ned's wanting to renege on an agreement we made. I thought we should talk it out."

"Well, hell, Jared. You can't make my job easy, can you."

"Look, this is all interesting, and I'd love to play guessing games with you, but I *have* to get on that plane. It's a matter of life and death."

"Now we're in perfect agreement. We just found Criswell dead. Shot with a nine millimeter."

Jared's body numbed. He had to ask. "Was Derek there? Is he dead, too?"

"Derek Hines?" Blake's brow crinkled in question. "No one mentioned him, but I've got a half-dozen witnesses who saw you two come to blows and heard you threaten to kill him. I have a warrant for your arrest for the murder of Ned Criswell."

A loud gasp escaped from the back of the SUV. Jared winced at the sound. Blake had to have heard her.

"Who's in the back of the truck?"

Jared wasn't about to have Courtney show her face. He pushed open the door and stepped onto the pavement.

Blake placed his hand on his weapon. "Whoever's in the back of the SUV, I want you out of the car, now. Hands up."

"She can't." Jared opened the door, held up his hands and stood toe-to-toe with the sheriff. "Damn it, Blake. You've known me since we were in high school. I wouldn't kill in cold blood."

"I thought so, too." Blake frowned. "You've

been a pain in my butt the last month with your theories about all those strange occurrences at your ranch. With no proof, I had no way to arrest Ned, and then you go and take things into your own hands. I expected more."

"You're not making any sense."

"How about if I spell it out. I have a list of complaints about sabotage on your ranch that simply stopped a couple of days ago. Not only that, you pulled every complaint and told my office they weren't valid. Even after the arson fire, not one request. But I know better. I saw the destroyed fences, the damage. We both know Criswell was probably involved. I even had a suspect. The guy's son, Chuck. And you go and refuse to assist in the investigation. You've never backed away from a fight in your life, and you just gave up. I've been wondering why."

Jared tilted his Stetson back and eyed the son of the man who'd tried to help him save Alyssa. He and Blake weren't really friends.

More like acquaintances. Not that he had any-thing against the sheriff, but he avoided any-thing that brought back those five-year-old memories. "Why did you pull me over?"

"Anonymous call that you were heading to the airport." The sheriff scowled at him. "You think I like doing this? I got word you've set your place up like a fortress, given guns to all your hands. Everyone's walking around armed, including the men delivering stock across state lines. What the hell's going on? If you tell me, I can help."

Jared shook his head. "You can't help. Any more than your father could five years ago. You have to trust me, Blake. I need to go. *We* need to go."

The sheriff pursed his lips. "Who's in the back of your truck?" he repeated.

"My nine-month-old son and his mother, and they're in danger."

Jared knew he couldn't have surprised Blake

more if he'd said he had a bunch of pink elephants in the backseat.

"Since when do you have a kid?" Blake said. "Now you have even more explaining to do."

"And I will, but right now you have to trust me."

"I'm sorry, Jared. I can't. Not with a warrant."

Jared leaned back against the car door and it clicked closed. "It wasn't me."

Blake pulled out his notes. "Look at it from my point of you. I have a fight over water, a confrontation, and the man was dead within a half hour of your leaving his ranch."

Jared let out a low curse. "Who the hell is doing this to us?" He glanced back at the SUV and took a couple of steps closer to the sheriff's vehicle so Courtney wouldn't hear them. He lowered his voice. "Look, I'm laying this on the line because I trusted your dad and by extension you. Someone threatened to kidnap and kill my son unless I paid a ransom. I have dozens of dead cattle, shots fired, an unexplained fire, and Velma was just attacked and is in the hospital. This is bigger than you and me. CTC is trying to help, but even they can't seem to pin this guy's identity down." Jared met Blake's gaze. "I know you have a family, and that you understand when someone is after them. I need you to let me go, Blake. I need to save *my* family."

The sheriff let out a low curse. "You're putting me in a tough position. I don't think you killed Ned, but we received a phone call from a witness who states he saw you do it. The judge issued the warrant. He's a fishing buddy of Ned's."

"What witness?"

"Anonymous call." Blake rubbed his temple. "I get it, but if I let you go, they'll arrest you somewhere else, and then where would your family be? At least here you have friends in your corner."

"No way. This guy has too much intel, Blake.

I have to get Courtney and Dylan out of Carder. If I don't I'll lose them."

"Bring them in. I'll help protect them."

"Five years ago I tried the right way." Jared shook his head. "This time I contacted a sure thing. All my men, CTC and high-tech surveillance couldn't protect them. I'm not sure why they're even still alive. I came too close to losing them. I can't trust anyone. I'm sorry."

The squeal of tires caused Jared to spin around. Léon's SUV peeled out and down the road.

"Courtney!"

"Let's go," Blake shouted. He rounded his vehicle then skidded to a halt. All four of his tires were flat.

"What the hell?"

Jared froze and squinted after the SUV. His entire body numb. Devastated, he looked over at Blake. "He has them. Damn it, Blake. Courtney and my son are gone."

THE SUV'S DOOR SLAMMED.

"Jared?" Courtney asked.

He didn't say anything, just gunned the accelerator. When the SUV took off, Courtney toppled backward. Dylan wailed and she grabbed the baby.

"Jared, can you slow down?"

"Your lover is long gone," a familiar whisper said.

She rose to her knees and peered over the middle row of seats. Her stomach plummeted. The back of the ski mask covered his hair.

"Stop. Please, let us out. I won't tell anyone."

"You should know better by now. My plans are not yours." The man looked over his shoulder and pointed a gun directly at her. "Sit down and shut up or you and your kid are dead. And don't bother trying to call Jared. I have a jammer blocking service. No one can help."

Would that stop the CTC team from tracking her, too? Maybe not. She'd leave the phone on, hoping they would find her. But she couldn't count on being rescued. She needed a plan.

Courtney made a show of backing off. She sat flat in the back of the SUV, holding Dylan close. The vehicle swerved and the road became rough. She bounced several inches off the floor. Where were they going?

Think, Courtney. Think.

She felt for her waist. The knife was there. She measured the distance between her and the man driving. The space was awkward. He would shoot her before she could cut him. In the vehicle the knife was useless.

If she could get his gun, she might have a chance. She'd simply have to look for an opportunity.

She pressed Dylan close to her and rocked him, but she couldn't calm him. What did she expect? Her own heart raced, her nerves were shot. She knew this man might very well kill them both.

The vehicle stopped. Courtney tensed. What was happening now? Was this the end?

"Don't move," he whispered. "You do, I kill the kid and leave you alive to know your mistake caused his death."

She shivered. He exited the car and locked them in. He seemed to be searching all around the car.

When he was finished he opened the door and knelt down searching below the dashboard. He grinned. "Your ace consultants saved me the trouble of removing the GPS chip. Ironic isn't it. They were trying to protect Jared and you, and they ended up making themselves blind."

"Why are you doing this?" she asked. Maybe if she figured out why, she could convince him.

He said nothing and started the vehicle, reversing direction. The SUV made another sharp turn and a slurry of mud rose in an arc.

Courtney could barely keep upright. Especially with Dylan in her arms.

When he stopped the SUV and opened the door she'd have to be ready.

She had no idea how long they drove, but the landscape hadn't changed. They pulled up to a small shack, the kind of isolated location where things never ended well.

Courtney gave Dylan a small kiss on his forehead. He looked up at her with so much trust. She prayed she could get them out of this alive. She prayed Jared would find her before anything worse happened.

The kidnapper exited the front and moved around the side. Courtney kept her hand at her waist and braced herself to attack. He yanked open the back end and she froze.

The man gripped an assault weapon in his hands.

She couldn't escape.

"Put the kid down," he whispered and threw her a rope.

"Get out of the SUV nice and easy," he said with a snarl.

She nodded.

"Excellent. You remember."

"Stand still and hold out your hands. If you try anything, I'll spray your kid with bullets."

She reached her hands out in front of her. He wrapped the rope around them and tied the knot off tight.

"Please, just let the baby go. He's innocent."

He slapped her across the face. "I told you no speaking. You have money and assume you don't have to follow the rules.

"Now walk."

She glanced at Dylan, hesitating. The spring heat was mild, but with the sun shining through the windshield, he'd burn up. "Please, the car will get too hot."

He slapped her across the cheek again. This time even harder. Her head whipped back and her jaw throbbed.

"Don't give me a reason, because it'll hurt

Jared just as much to spray this car with bullets and kill you both."

"He could fall."

He hit her a third time, but walked back to close the back door.

"Thank you."

The man raised his hand to hit her. She recoiled and he chuckled. "The kid is Jared's son. That makes him my most valuable asset. I've been waiting years to finish what I started five years ago."

She gasped in shock at the realization. Oh my God. This wasn't about her father at all. This was the man who killed Jared's wife and daughter.

Her throat clenched. No one had seen it. The money must've been a diversion the entire time.

And now he planned to kill her and Dylan.

"I see in your eyes you've finally figured it out. That's better than Jared ever did. He never understood. Never realized I should have had everything."

He lifted the weapon. "Now walk."

She made her way to the door of the shack. "Open it."

Using both hands she twisted the doorknob and the rotting wood swung inward. She turned her head sideways, trying to see behind the mask, to make out who would do this. She couldn't tell except that behind the ski mask his eyes were flat and dead. He showed no mercy in his expression.

"Go inside and sit in the chair."

She walked in and sat down. The knife burned at her waist, but in her head every scenario she came up with ended in Dylan's bullet-riddled body.

There had to be a way to save her son.

"Stay in the chair. If you move, I kill your son. If you speak, I kill your son. If you beg, I kill your son. Do you understand?"

She nodded.

He returned a few moments later with Dylan and the car seat. He strapped the baby in and left him to cry.

She winced, but he seemed impervious to her child's screams.

Courtney worked her hands against the sturdy rope as surreptitiously as possible. At one point he whirled around and glared at her, staring at the tie.

He picked up the weapon and walked over to the car seat. She sucked in a deep breath and he smiled at her.

She got the message. He controlled everything.

Courtney couldn't move. She couldn't call for help. She couldn't try to convince him to let her go. She couldn't reach the knife.

She and Dylan were well and truly trapped.

Chapter Twelve

His ranch house had turned into a mausoleum. Every instinct screamed to search the roads, the mountains, the ranch, everywhere, but he had no leads.

He wandered from room to room, but in every square foot a crisp memory of Dylan's laughter or Courtney's smile would haunt him. He stopped by the guest room. His eyes closed in pain at the view of the crib. He moved down the hall to the kitchen. A plate of snickerdoodles sat there, lonely and pathetic.

Finally, he pushed through the large mahogany study doors. Where she'd shared with him the danger she and Dylan were in. Where he'd vowed to save her. Where they'd made love for the second time.

Courtney and Dylan had changed his life the moment she'd driven onto his land in that powder blue Mustang. He'd been dead inside for so long, he'd never even realized it. She'd dragged him kicking and screaming back to life. Right now he wondered if that was a good or a bad thing.

Velma would say good. Roscoe would say bad. For Jared, the jury was still out.

What Courtney had done was make him feel again. She'd brought him hope, he'd dared to believe in the possibilities, and now she and Dylan were gone. The feelings remained, though, except instead of a warmth inside, it was dark and ice laden.

The worst part, they'd been a half mile from getting out of Texas and regrouping. So close. Jared had been standing just feet away.

How had the guy pulled it off? Jared should

have been able to protect them. He might never be able to forgive himself. When he and Blake had realized they wouldn't be able to follow, and that the nearest deputy was twenty minutes away, Jared had known he'd been beaten. That he'd failed. Despite the planning and preparation and the determination.

He was at a madman's mercy.

Jared circled the room, but there wasn't an inch that Courtney and Jared hadn't touched.

He had to get them back.

He stopped at the coffee table across from the couch. The cell phone the kidnapper had left with Courtney lay there, taunting him. Jared stared at it unblinking. Would the man even call?

He slipped the phone in his pocket. It was a call he couldn't afford to miss. "He must have seen me leave with Courtney and Dylan and decided to switch up his plan, though I don't know how." Jared looked over at Léon. "What's your gut tell you?"

"That's why we're looking at an inside job with a high tech expert. Too much has gone wrong. I've got my men interviewing every member of the staff again. Zane's executing a deep dive. If there's something there, we'll find it." The operative frowned and Jared's gut twisted in fear.

Jared rubbed his eyes. "I hope the guy's just greedy. He can have the money if he'll let Courtney and Dylan go."

"Me, too, Jared. Me, too."

But Jared could read the man's eyes. They were cautious and wary. Jared wouldn't ask for odds. He didn't want to know because he refused to let himself consider the alternative. He *would* find Courtney and Dylan. He would bring them back safe and sound, and then he'd send them as far away from Last Chance Ranch and Carder as quickly as possible so they could live their lives in peace.

"How long have we been waiting?" Jared asked, rubbing the back of his neck.

"Two hours."

Léon's tone didn't evoke optimism. They all knew the truth. Unless they caught a break, the guy was in charge. They needed him to call.

A knock sounded at the front door. Léon left the study to answer it.

"Can I see him?"

Jared tensed at Blake Redmond's voice. The man couldn't apologize enough. Jared wished he could blame the sheriff, but there was nothing the man could have done to stop the abduction, except to never have stopped the SUV in the first place. Okay, so maybe he blamed Blake a bit. But the truth was, Jared knew the only one at fault was himself. He should've taken them into the mountains when his gut was screaming at him to do so.

The sheriff entered the room, hat in hand. His boots scuffed across the floor. "Any news?"

Jared shook his head. "No note, no ransom, no call. No nothing."

"Damn, I'm sorry." Blake frowned. "I have more bad news, unfortunately. We found Derek's truck abandoned near the Criswell place. I'm sorry to say we found blood on the back of the seat."

"Not an accident."

Blake shook head. "Sorry."

Jared braced himself. God, how was he going to tell Roscoe? "And Derek."

"We don't know. My deputies are still searching. Maybe he wondered off, disoriented from his injury."

"Why am I not surprised?" Jared met Blake's gaze. "The guy has been ahead of us from the start. He's been toying with us since he wrote the note."

Léon entered the room with a duffel. "Here's the money. When he calls we'll be ready to make the drop."

Jared froze at the sight. He clamped his jaw shut. Five years vanished in the space of a heartbeat. Steeling himself, he opened the bag and stared at the bundles of cash.

"This still doesn't make sense. Did whoever come up with this scheme want money, and want Jamison to lose his family? Is this about revenge? Why focus everything on me."

"You've got the money." Léon twisted his lips into a frown. "But you're right. Nothing fits. It's all off. Zane investigated all the employees who lost their jobs because of the mill going under. No one lost a close family member."

"We're missing something," Jared said. "Something that's right in front of us."

"It feels like a diversion," Léon said. "Similar to the fire. He didn't leave any kind of trace evidence, either here or on the highway. He's a ghost."

Jared paced back and forth. A ghost. The déjà vu feeling made Jared nauseous. He glared at the phone. "Why don't you call?" he shouted.

The front door rattled with the sound of a key entering the dead bolt. Jared palmed his Glock and stood in the hallway waiting.

Tim escorted a limping figure into the foyer. Jared slipped the pistol back into the holster and strode over to the foreman. "Roscoe. Getting out of bed was a damn fool thing to do."

Jared patted his shoulder. "I know, but she's a survivor. She'll pull out of this."

"Of course she will," Roscoe said. "She's not through mothering the lot of us. Any news?"

Jared shook his head, avoiding his foreman's gaze. He wouldn't tell him about Derek yet. Not until they knew more.

Roscoe cleared his throat. "Courtney's tough and determined. She'll come out of this. So will that boy."

Jared tamped down his emotions. "I believe that, but I'm a little surprised to hear those words coming from you."

"City girls can grow on you," Roscoe said, glancing away.

"Since when?" Jared asked.

"Since a gal from New York schooled me on assuming the worst." He adjusted his cane. "She's a keeper."

If things were different, Jared would move heaven and earth to convince her to stay once he found her. But that wasn't where he saw the night ending.

He only saw an empty house, an empty bed and an empty life. He had every intention of saving her and then letting her go to keep her safe.

He lowered his head and rubbed the sting from his eye.

A grandmother clock chimed. Outside, dusk had begun to darken the sky. "Where are you? Courtney? Please be okay."

The phone in his pocket vibrated. The *kidnapper's* phone.

He grabbed it and pressed the speakerphone. "King."

For a moment he heard nothing.

"Jared King," the voice whispered. "It's been a long time."

His gaze flew to Léon's. "Do I know you?"

"Perhaps you'll recognize me this way." There was a pause over the phone. "You didn't follow the rules. Again. You haven't learned anything. Five years ago or now."

That mechanized voice. Jared's legs shook and he stumbled into the study. He sank into the chair so his legs would hold him. Impossible. Five years ago. It was *him*. The man who had killed Alyssa.

"Surprise," he said. "Did you miss me?"

"You son of a bitch."

"I like the title, but it's not true. My mother was a saint."

"Shall we return to unfinished business. I didn't receive my payment five years ago. I tacked on interest this time."

Jared glanced over at Léon. What the hell was going on? They'd figured out where the odd amount came from. Edward Jamison."

Léon shook his head.

"You're confused, are you? Don't be. I may have tweaked the numbers a bit just for fun when I realized our game wasn't over. You were a naughty boy, going to New York, falling for *another* girl. Getting her pregnant."

"Who are you?" How had he known? Courtney had only come to him a few days ago. "You don't have to do this. Courtney and Dylan are innocent."

The voice chuckled, and the inhuman sound made him shiver. "But you aren't."

Jared thrust his hand through his hair. "What do you want?"

"Oh, I'm getting exactly what I want. You know I could hang up and just let that be the end. I suppose you might find them. Someday."

"What about your money?"

"There is that."

A long pause made Jared want to leap through the phone and strangle the guy. Léon came up beside Jared and pressed the mute button. "I know you want to challenge him," the operative said. "Don't. He wants to be in charge. Let him. We still haven't identified him, and if Jamison isn't involved, Zane's search has been one giant waste of time. You need to do whatever it takes to have this meet."

Jared gave a curt nod. "I know. But when I'm near the guy, I'm not holding back."

"Jared. I think it's time we have a reunion. How about we take a walk down memory lane. Bring the money to the pier at Last Chance Lake. You have one hour. And leave your little friends at home. If I see the sheriff or those spies you tried to hire leave your house, she and your son are dead."

"Wait—"

The call ended. Jared sent Léon a desperate look. "Could you trace it?"

The CTC operative shook his head. "He timed it perfectly. We only needed three more seconds. We did get that he's probably in the county."

"Of course he is. He'll be at the lake in an hour." Jared shook his head. "We're out of options. He's looking for an excuse to kill them." He looked around the room from man to man. "Either I'm going alone, or it has to *look* like I'm going alone. I won't take any chances with their lives. Not this time."

León frowned. "We don't have much time to put any fail safes in place. He could be there already. Watching and waiting."

Jared's frowned deepened. "Which is why this time, I'm going to do exactly what he says."

A SLIVER OF red sky lined the horizon. It was getting dark. She could only make out the boat sitting near a platform at the center of the lake.

Her son was strapped to his car seat in that boat, the kidnapper sitting right beside him holding a pistol. Dylan was completely vulnerable, completely at his mercy.

So was she. Because she would do anything to keep Dylan safe.

Courtney sat in the wooden chair her masked kidnapper had placed on the end of the pier. Her hands were still bound and since he'd left her, she'd been working her wrists against the strong hemp. She could feel the blood dripping off her fingertips.

He'd strapped a heavy weight belt to her waist, but she could stand up if she wanted. Except the moment she moved off this chair, he'd shoot her son.

He was in control.

The baby had been screaming for close to an hour. She winced at the loud hiccups.

"Ma. Ma," he sobbed. "Ma. Ma."

They were in big trouble. She had to find a way to save herself and her son, but she had no idea how to do that.

The rumble of an engine dragged her attention away from her thoughts. Her heart skipped a beat, reigniting hope within her.

Jared's old truck pulled up to the edge of the pier. He jumped out with a duffel bag.

His eyes widened when he saw her, and then his gaze whipped toward the sound of their crying son in the boat. He walked down the pier, his face obscured by the darkening sky.

Even then she'd never seen him so tense, strained, or so angry.

"I'm sorry," she said, not sure if he could hear her.

"Stop," the kidnapper's mechanized voice ordered through a bullhorn once Jared had made it halfway down the wooden planks.

Courtney kept working her wrists. With the man distracted, maybe she could reach the knife. The problem was, any wrong move and he *would* kill Dylan.

Jared lifted the bag. "Here's the money. I came alone. How about we end this now? You take the money. We forget this ever happened. Just let them go."

The man pointed the barrel of a pistol at the car seat. "I don't think so."

"No. Please don't," Courtney shouted, desperately wanting to stand and beg, but knowing if she moved, Dylan's life was forfeit. He'd warned her enough when he'd forced her to sit in that chair.

"Shut up," the kidnapper ordered. "Or I kill him anyway."

Her gaze flew to Jared's. *He's not bluffing*, she mouthed. *He's crazy. He will do it.*

"I know," Jared said as quietly as he could. He exuded a calm confidence she didn't think she would ever feel again. She prayed he had a plan.

He lifted his chin, his expression determined and indomitable. He *did*. He had something in mind.

"Here's the way we play this game, Jared. A little different from five years ago, isn't it?

You have two people you love. Two people you want to save.

"But you can't save them both." The man chuckled. "You have a choice. But first things first. There's a small boat right off the pier next to your lover. Put the money in it."

Jared walked the remainder of the way on the pier and lowered the duffel into the fiberglass craft.

He was within reach of her and she looked up at him. He was tall and strong and she couldn't imagine anyone she'd trust more to save their son.

"Excellent," the kidnapper said.

A small motor burst to life and the remote-controlled boat puttered across the lake, past the swimming platform, heading toward the opposite edge.

"You have what you want, let them go," Jared said. He paused. "Please."

"I don't have near what I want. We haven't finished our transaction."

Courtney's gut hurt at the malevolence in the man's voice. She closed her eyes. *Please. Save Dylan.*

"I control you. Your every move. I have what you want. Finally. What I should have had from the beginning."

"Who are you?" Jared asked.

"Your conscience. Your nightmare?" The man chuckled. "It doesn't matter who I am. What matters is you will always remember this moment. Because you will have to live with your choice."

Dylan's cries grew softer, more tired.

"Sounds like your kid wants this to be over. So do I. It's time to choose. Your lover or your son."

"No, you can't do that!" Courtney shouted.

"I'm in control. I can do whatever I want." His mechanized laughter filtered across the water from the boat. "You can save one of them. If you choose the baby. I leave him here on the platform for you to save, but you, you must push her in the water and let her go. If you try to save her, your son will die.

"If you choose her, I throw the kid into the water and he drowns."

He lifted a heavy dumbbell tied to rope. It was attached to the car seat.

Jared's entire body froze, but she could see the agony in his eyes.

"You don't have to do this," he said. "You have the money. Please. I'm begging you. What do I have to do?"

"I like you begging me, Jared. Makes you humble." The man laughed. "Would you give me everything you have? Your money, the house, the land, the oil?"

"Take it all." Jared's voice had grown desperate. "Whatever you want. Just let them live."

"Get on your knees. Beg me."

Jared didn't hesitate. He hit the wooden pier as if in prayer. "I'm begging you. Do whatever you want to do to me. Just let them go."

Tears streamed down Courtney's face. This

wasn't what either of them had expected. There was no way they were getting out of this alive.

The man just laughed. Then suddenly he stopped.

"Choose. Now. If you don't make the choice, I'll shoot the boy, then her. You'll lose them both."

Jared stood up. He looked at Courtney, then at his son. She could tell he was weighing his chances of saving them both.

The distance was too great. This was impossible.

"You betting I can't hit her? Think again. The pistol might suck for accuracy." The man held up a rifle. "It's not that tough of a shot."

The words ended Courtney's hope for herself. A strange peace swept through her body. She raised her gaze to the man she'd grown to love, the man who would sacrifice his life for them if he could.

"Jared." Courtney's voice was calm. "You

have to save Dylan. He's all that matters. We agreed."

He stared at her, his eyes frantic. "I can save you both," he muttered under his breath. "I promise."

"I have faith in you." Courtney swallowed. "But I don't trust him."

She shifted slightly and her eyes welled. She blinked. "I never told you this, but I love you, Jared. From the moment we met."

"Courtney—"

"You're a good father," she said. "Please tell Dylan that I loved him with all my heart."

With that one statement, Courtney stood and jumped into the water, sinking like a stone.

Chapter Thirteen

Jared watched in horror as Courtney disappeared beneath the water. He knew with the weight around her waist she'd disappear below the surface and end up on the bottom of the twenty-five-foot expanse.

This couldn't be happening again. The man sitting in the boat cursed. "Damn her. I wanted you to make the choice!"

A shot rang out. The man fell to the side. Dylan screamed.

Jared's gaze flew to Léon's location two hundred yards as the crow flies. It had been an unbelievable shot, but Léon was a pro.

Blake Redmond raced from his hiding place

across the lake and commandeered a wait-ing boat.

Knowing his child would be safe in mo-ments, Jared yanked off his boots and dove into the water. The lake was lower than normal and murky. The last bit of light muted even more as he swam down to the cold depths. He squinted, barely able to make out strange shadowy shapes.

A horrifying sense of déjà vu nearly suffo-cated him. This time it would end differently. Desperate, Jared reached out for the base of the pier. She'd gone down right beside it. He could follow the post.

His hand encountered a thick wooden sup-port and he used it as a guide. Down deeper and deeper he dove. His lungs protested but Jared wasn't about to go back up for air. Not without Courtney.

Darkness engulfed him.

No. This wasn't happening again. Not like

before. Suddenly, out of nowhere he made out a murky figure hunched in the water. He kicked to her and clutched her arm. She shook him away and he realized she was using the knife he'd given her to free herself from the weighted belt. He shoved her hands to the side, pulled out his combat knife and finished the job.

The belt fell free. She slumped forward and grew heavy in his arms.

Don't do this, Courtney.

He wrapped his arm around her waist and kicked for all he could to the surface. He broke through the water and sucked in a deep breath. Her turned her in his arms and his heart sank back down to the lake's floor.

She was limp in his arms.

"Give her to me," Léon shouted above him. The CTC operative leaned over the pier, hands outstretched. Jared lifted her up and Léon dragged her onto the wooden platform.

He rolled her over just as Jared climbed onto the pier.

"She was moving just seconds ago," he shouted, moving to Courtney's side.

Jared bent over her. "Come on, Courtney."

He turned her head to the side and some water escaped her mouth. "That's it," he urged. He placed his hands on her neck and waited for the beat of life.

Nothing. He had to get her heart started.

He placed his hands over her heart and started compressions. Ten, twenty beats.

No. This couldn't be happening. He tilted her head back. "Courtney, you've got a son who needs you. I need you."

He breathed into her mouth. Once, twice, and felt for her pulse. Was that a small thready sign of life?

A bolt of energy washed over him. "You can do it. Fight. For Dylan."

He rested his cheek against her lips. Still no air movement.

He puffed in another two breaths. Then two more.

He turned her to her side and pounded her back.

Her lungs heaved. Water spewed from her mouth and she jerked against him. She turned on her side expelling the water from her lungs.

Léon looked at Jared a wide grin on his face. "Hallelujah."

Jared bent over Courtney and cupped her face in his hands. "Welcome back," he whispered softly.

She blinked up at him. "Dylan?"

"Safe." He pointed at the swimming platform in the center of the lake. Blake held their still-crying son in his arms.

She sagged against him, her shaky arms winding around him. "I—"

Jared helped her sit up and pulled her close.

"Are you crazy?" He squeezed her tight. "Don't ever do that again."

She looked up at him again. "Wouldn't you have done the same?"

"That's not the point." He glared at her, then rocked her close to him, kissing her temple, her cheeks and finally her lips. "I almost lost you."

"I know." Her voice was thick with emotion. "But you didn't. You saved our son. You saved us both."

She opened her clenched hand. The folded knife lay in her palm.

"You cut the way through most of the strap," Jared said. "I don't know if I could have gotten you out in time."

"I had to fight. For you. For our son. I knew you'd save Dylan even if I didn't make it, but the truth is, you need me. I haven't even showed you how to change a diaper yet."

She smiled at him and lay her head softly against his chest. "Thank you."

Jared nodded to Léon. "Tell Ransom, thank you."

"This will be one for the record books."

They all watched as Blake maneuvered the boat toward them. The soft growl of the drew closer, the remote control craft with the duffel of money floating behind.

The boat tapped the edge of the pier. Dylan reached up to Jared and he grabbed the boy in his arms, hugging him tightly before handing him over to Courtney.

She held him close, checking every inch. "Jelly Bean."

"Mama," he hiccupped.

"He's okay."

She held her son close and Jared wrapped his arms around both of them. His cheek rested against her hair. He closed his eyes and said a thankful prayer.

A thud drew his attention. Blake and Léon

had moved the body to the pier. He lay there, still masked and anonymous, half the back of his head was gone.

"I had to take the head shot so he couldn't pull the trigger on reflex," Léon said.

"Who is it?" Jared asked. "Who hated me enough to kill the innocent."

Blake knelt beside the body and peeled the ski mask up.

Jared gasped. His knees gave way.

"No. It can't be." He shook his head back and forth at the very familiar face.

"Derek Hines?" He shook his head back and forth. "He was my best friend for years. I trusted him with my life. We had him guarding the house."

The lapping of the water against the pier was the only sound for several minutes.

"Why? Why would he do this?"

THE SMALL CARDER hospital was going to drive her crazy. Courtney lay in the bed. Every doctor, nurse and staffer had found a reason to visit.

A teenage candy striper poked her head through the door. "Do you need anything, ma'am?" she asked with a giggle.

"Thank you, no."

She fought not to snap. The residents of Carder were doing everything in their power to make her feel at home. Actually, it was too much of a good thing.

She glanced over at Jared and he chuckled. "I could put up a do-not-disturb sign."

"Do you think it would work?" She couldn't stop the hope from lingering in her voice.

"Not a chance. You're famous," he said. "The woman who was willing to give her life for her son." All humor left Jared's face. "I'm sorry I put you in that position. I should never have let it get that far."

"It's not your fault. It's his," Courtney said, wishing she could wipe the guilt from his face. He'd made it possible for her to save herself and then he'd saved her. Didn't he understand they were in this together?

"Doctor says I can leave as soon as he finishes my paperwork," she said, hoping for a response.

Jared nodded and patted Dylan's back. He adjusted his position a bit. Dylan lay against his shoulder, perfectly content to be in his father's arms. "He looks good in your arms," she murmured.

Jared glanced down at the baby. "I can't stop looking at him, checking his fingers and toes, watching him breathe."

"I felt that way every day for a long time after I brought him home from the hospital."

"So I'll get used to it?" he asked.

She shook her head. "No. Because he's a miracle."

"You both are." Jared cleared his throat. "We've never talked about it, but I'm sorry I wasn't there for you, when you were pregnant, when you gave birth to him. I hope you know I would have been there. If you'd wanted me."

"I know," she said. "I'm sorry you missed out on so much."

Jared brushed a lock of hair from the baby's forehead. "He likes horses."

"I'm not surprised."

Courtney kept silent. She could see he wanted to say something, and her entire body shimmered with anticipation.

Were they thinking the same thing? How was she supposed to get around to asking the question she longed to ask?

She breathed in deeply. She'd just have to do it. If the last few days had taught her one thing it was not to wait, but to grab on to life with both hands and shove fear aside. Carpe diem. Seize the day had never become more real.

Before she could, a sharp knock sounded at the door and Léon walked into her room with another man.

"This is Zane Westin, CTC's ace computer

whiz, in the flesh. He's been delving into Derek Hines's secret life. The man kept meticulous notes, obsessively so. I thought you'd want to know what we've discovered, but first I wanted to make certain you knew that the BOLO's been rescinded. You won't be arrested if you travel to New York."

Courtney's gaze flew to Jared. Even in the celebration of returning to the ranch, Jared had been tortured. Roscoe was inconsolable. Neither of them could understand why Derek could've been the man behind that ski mask.

"Secret life?" Jared asked.

"Everything he told you and his father since he left the military was a lie," Zane said. "He never earned a degree, but he did run some cons and he was good at ferreting out information." Zane glanced back and forth between Courtney and Jared.

"Tell them," Léon said.

"He's been obsessed for a long time with your family and your ranch." Zane pulled out a file folder. "Jared, he met your first wife in a bar the week before you did. From his writings he thought he was in love with her."

"Strange. I remember we went to the bar together when I met Alyssa." Jared's brow wrinkled in confusion. "He never said anything."

"Evidently, she fell hard for you, when his intention had been to show her off," Zane commented. "He wrote dozens of draft emails in his system, letters he never sent to her, begging her for a chance, threatening you to leave her alone. When he finally sent one of the emails, she didn't remember him. Once she chose you, it sent him over the edge. When you married something inside of him snapped. He blamed you for everything in his life that didn't work."

"This doesn't make sense. We were friends. We confided in each other."

"He kept a lot of secrets and they burned a hole in his gut. He never told anyone. He believed his father would rather have had you for a son. He became obsessed with taking everything away from you. When Chuck Criswell started his destruction campaign, Derek took a lot of pleasure in our investigation. He took the shot at Angel Maker to spook the horse. He had no idea the pin had been removed and the bull would get out. He found the irony amusing. He also salted the water and gassed the quarter horse barns."

"He almost killed his own father."

"Collateral damage would be acceptable, he wrote."

Jared rubbed his eyes. "Why didn't I see it?"

"He didn't want you to. And he wasn't around enough for you to pick up on the inconsistencies of his behavior. I called a few of the guys he hung out with. They said everyone talked about how the guy was just off enough to make them nervous."

"How did he find out about me?" Courtney asked.

"When your private investigator began the

search for Jared, it clued Derek in. It's one thing he didn't lie about. He was actually gifted. Even Zane was impressed. Once he realized through your PI that your father was in financial trouble, his plan took shape. He hacked into the bank and adjusted their records. The bank believed a decision had been made to call in the loans. They believed the notes in the computer. Most people do. Derek manipulated the situation so you'd have to ask Jared for help. Derek hired a thug to kill Botelli because the PI was a loose end he couldn't risk."

"Derek set up this elaborate scheme just to get back at me?" Jared's incredulous voice was tinged with hurt.

"A five-year-long plan to destroy you. He was simply waiting for the right opportunity to hurt you as much has he had been," Zane said. "Impressive for a crazy guy."

Léon shot Zane a pointed look. The man shrugged. "What? It's the truth."

Courtney had a hard time processing all the information. She'd been a pawn in a revenge plot that had started years ago? She shifted in the bed. Everything they'd been through had been orchestrated by one man searching for revenge.

"One last thing you both need to know," Léon said. "His plan from the start was to get Courtney and the baby out to that lake to kill them both. He never wanted the money. He blamed his lack of money on losing Alyssa, but he actually wanted to drive you insane. Once you cracked after losing them, he planned to swoop in to take over the ranch.

"He wanted your life."

A small choked gasp sounded from the doorway. Roscoe swayed. Léon rushed over and propped the old man up.

Jared rose and placed Dylan in Courtney's arms. He walked over to Roscoe and stared at the foreman. The man's eyes were bloodshot and he looked ten years older than he had when she'd last spoken to him.

"I didn't know." He clutched Jared's shirt. "I swear. I didn't know."

Jared nodded. "Neither of us knew."

Roscoe stared at his feet. He looked at Courtney, to Dylan and back to Jared. "I... I'm so very sorry."

He limped out the door. Jared started to follow. Léon held him back. "Leave him be. It takes time when you discover you've been betrayed by those closest to you."

Jared thrust his hand through his hair. "The irony is, if Derek had wanted to run the ranch with me, I'd have let him. I loved him like a brother. What does that say that I couldn't see what he was. What he'd done."

"He was a functioning sociopath," Zane said. "He knew how society would expect him to behave, but the truth is the world revolved around Derek Hines and that's all he could see. There was nothing you could have done or said. He had no empathy for anyone."

Jared stretched out his hand to shake Léon's, then Zane's. "Thank you. Both of you. Tell Ransom I owe him more than I can ever repay."

"I'm glad we could help," Léon said. "I'm glad it turned out well for you all."

Léon smiled at Courtney and she glanced down at her baby boy. "Thank you for saving his life."

He gave her a kiss on the cheek before he and Zane headed out.

Jared walked back to Courtney.

"Are you okay?" she asked softly, gently rocking Dylan.

He sat on the edge of her bed. "No. I keep thinking back from the time Derek arrived on the ranch. I did trust him with my life. I would have trusted him with yours. I *did* trust him with yours, with everyone's life."

He met her gaze. "I'm so sorry for everything. For all the pain you went through." He swallowed. "I know you're probably ready to get out of Carder and go back to New York." He looked down at Dylan and placed his hand on the boy's head. "I… I'll do whatever you want, but I'd like to be part of his life. If you'll let me."

Courtney froze. She hadn't expected him to kick her out. She'd hoped… She turned her face to the side, away from him.

"Why are you doing this?"

"You have a life in New York. A career. Your father. Why would you want to stay here? It's just a reminder of how badly everything could have turned out."

Even as the words echoed from his lips, Courtney's back tensed. She looked him straight in the eye.

"Is this what you really want?"

"It's for the best. I'll talk to Ransom about using the plane to fly you back to New York. We'll figure out something."

"Jared. Why?"

"Because it's the right thing."

THE SUN WAS setting on Last Chance Ranch. Jared stood on the porch while Courtney packed. The plane was ready and he would soon say goodbye.

Roscoe guided Velma's wheelchair from inside. Jared knelt down in front of her. "How are you doing today?"

"Irritated," she muttered. "Can't button my clothes, can't cook. Can't stand up without getting dizzy." She gazed at Roscoe. "I'm sorry about Derek."

"I still can't believe it," Roscoe said with a weighed frown.

Velma patted Roscoe's hand. "He was sick in the head. Something happened to him, Roscoe. It wasn't your fault. Don't forget that."

"I'm not so sure about that. I don't know if I'll ever be."

The wound was fresh and raw and they all

felt it. Rain clouds filled the sky to the west. The perfect ending to what would be a horrible day Jared would remember until he was dead and buried in the ground.

"I'm walking over to the east," Jared said.

He didn't have to say where he was going. Roscoe and Velma would know. And understand.

Angel Maker snorted as he walked past the bull, but he ignored the stud. He was numb.

A white fence surrounded the small family cemetery. Jared stood in front of the two newest crosses. Alyssa's and his daughter's.

"We caught him, honey. God I'm sorry I didn't see it. I keep thinking back when I introduced you. Why didn't I see shock or anger on his face? Why didn't I see how much he hated me?"

He crouched down in front of the grave and pulled a weed.

"I wanted to save you, Alyssa. I wanted us to be a family." He sighed. "You'd have liked

Courtney, though. You two could have talked shopping and shoes for days. I almost lost her, too. I don't know how she survived, but I know I have to let her go. Even though she told me she loved me, it's for the best."

"Do you really believe that?" Courtney's voice was laced with hurt and sorrow.

Jared rose to his feet and turned to face her. She was alone.

"Where's Dylan?" he asked.

"With Velma and Roscoe, eating a snickerdoodle."

"Are you packed?"

She lifted her chin. "No."

He blinked. "I don't understand."

"I've been up all night thinking about leaving you. I need to know one thing. Why. Why let us go?"

"I… I—"

"I thought so. You love us, Jared King. Deny it and I'll walk out of here without looking back. We'll do the court thing, the visitation rights and move on. You can see Dylan every other Christmas and a couple weeks in the summer."

He rubbed his face with his hands and led her away from the graveyard. The ranch house and barn loomed in the distance. "This isn't your kind of place, Courtney. Admit it. Would you have ever come to Carder if you hadn't been desperate?"

"If I'd known you'd lived here, I'd have at least visited." She frowned at him. "Why are you making all these assumptions? Since when did I deserve to be pushed into a cookie-cutter life because of who my father is or what hotel I like to stay or even where I work, because you know what, Jared. You're not *just* a cowboy. I learned that a long time ago. You're an entrepreneur, you're a risk taker, and when it comes to me and my son, you're a hero."

His mouth gaped.

"So I've decided you've been in charge for

too long," Courtney said. "I think you could do with a shake-up in your life, Mr. King."

A flicker of hope ignited in Jared's belly, but he quickly tamped it down. What was she saying?

"You wouldn't have chosen to live here."

"Nope." Courtney looked around. "Until a few days ago I'd never heard of Carder, Texas. This was never my primary destination. But things change. People change. Do you recognize what you have in this small town?" She stepped closer to him. "When you were in trouble, no one bargained or even questioned whether they would help. They just did. Your men put their lives on the line to guard me and Dylan, two people they didn't even know."

She leaned into him. "I only knew one person in my building, and that was Marilyn. Her family won't accept my call. Even though CTC provided the police with the evidence I wasn't involved with her death. The rest of the building, except for the doorman, they probably don't even know my name. I could walk down the street right next to my building and no one would *see* me, much less know me.

"Look how everyone has rallied around Roscoe, despite what Derek did. You have a gift, and I want Dylan to be cherished the same way the people of this community cherish you. I've felt more like part of a family here on this ranch than I have since my mother died."

With a sigh, she placed her hand on his cheek. "I didn't know what I was missing without you in my life. Now that I recognize it, I can't go back to what I was. I've changed, Jared. Our son changed my life. And you changed it. I want to stay. Here. With you."

Jared could barely breathe. His legs shook and he cupped her face. "Are you certain? We lived through hell. Normal won't be exciting or intriguing."

"That's okay. I can do normal. I'd love to do normal."

Jared felt the ice around his heart—the barrier that had frozen him that horrible night five years ago—melt away.

He gripped her hands in his. "The night I met you, I could barely speak. I needed a shot of tequila to give me the courage to walk up to you. It was the best decision of my life.

"I want you to know that you brought me back to life. I was dead inside until you lit a spark."

She smiled at him, her heart shining in her face. "Finally." She gripped his shirt. "And I knew you were different the moment you approached me. I just didn't understand why you were so much more than anyone I'd ever met." Courtney pressed herself against him. "I didn't know what I'd been missing." She smiled. "Then Dylan came along and he showed me. He and you are the best things that ever happened to me."

She slipped her arms around his waist and rested her head on his chest.

Jared sighed in contentment. "I want you to be happy."

She leaned back. "You're not responsible for my happiness, Jared. But know this. I can find happy here. With you."

"You're going to stay?"

"If I'm asked the right way."

Jared grinned. "Miss Jamison, will you stay with me on the Last Chance Ranch?"

She pretended to consider the offer. "I could be convinced."

She lifted her lips to his and his heart sang when he kissed her back. He held out his hand and she threaded her fingers through his. "So, we take this last chance together?" he asked.

"We'll make it work, Jared. I believe that."

"And I believe in you," he said, taking her lips once more. "Always."

Epilogue

The West Texas sunset flared with a mass of color, orange and pink, purple and blue painting the violet sky. Jared paced the front porch of his house. He couldn't stop the nerves from twisting his gut.

If he'd learned one thing about Courtney over the last few months, she liked to plan and she didn't always appreciate surprises.

"What was I thinking?" he muttered under his breath. The entire event had seemed like a good idea at the time.

Now he wasn't so sure.

He tugged at his shirt collar.

"Are you going to cut and run, my friend?" Léon posed, dropping any pretext of hiding his accent.

"No more hiding," Jared said. "But I may have made a mistake. Maybe a trip home to New York..."

"Do you love her?" Léon asked.

"More than my life." More than he'd ever imagined. She deserved something more extravagant.

"Then it's no mistake. If I've learned anything over the last few years, it's that home isn't a place. For you, or for her. Besides, didn't she say she wanted to stay."

Jared shoved his hands into his pocket. "After she got out of the hospital. She was grateful. She could change her mind. Why wouldn't she?"

Léon let out a strange word, but even if Jared didn't understand the language, he knew a curse when he heard one.

The screen door opened and Courtney

peeked outside. Her gaze landed on Léon. "Weren't you heading back to Dallas?" she said.

"Thought I might hang around, see if I can't find a place to rest my hat for a while," the man replied, his unique accent melting away, being replaced by a perfect Texas drawl. Léon let very few into the secrets of his life.

He briefly met Jared's gaze and wandered toward the barn.

"Is he okay?" Courtney asked, slipping into Jared's embrace and wrapping her arms around him.

"Someday, I hope."

He swallowed and tightened his embrace. He rested his cheek against her hair and inhaled the fresh scent. Her softness sank into him. He never wanted to be a day without feeling this way.

"He deserves it. He's lonely, isn't he?"

Jared pulled away slightly and met her gaze. "You see to the heart of people, don't you?"

"Not really," Courtney said. "I have a lot of flaws, Jared."

"I don't recognize them. Besides, you saw through me, no matter how much I tried to protect myself from you and Dylan."

"You were hurting." She sighed and met his gaze. "Is Roscoe still planning to leave?"

Jared scowled at the barn. "I can't convince him to stay. Velma's beside herself. She's done everything she can, but he blames himself for not seeing how twisted Derek had become."

Courtney clasped his arm. "You have to stop him. He's family."

"Well, I disabled his truck, so we have one more shot."

Her eyes widened "You didn't."

"He's not leaving without a fight."

"That's what I love about you, Jared King. You don't give up without a fight." She reached up to kiss him.

Jared closed his eyes and returned her touch.

His heart raced. It was time. He held out his hand. "Come with me?"

She placed her hand into his. "Where are we going?"

"A surprise," he muttered beneath his breath. He led her over to the barn and slid open the door.

"Surprise!"

A cacophony of shouts greeted them. Courtney's eyes widened with shock. She gripped his hand tight. Her eyes teared up. Her gaze moved across all their family and friends. Blake Redmond and his wife and their children. Ransom and his family, the rest of the CTC operatives. Léon stood in the corner, alone but with a slight smile on his face.

She opened her mouth to speak when her gaze fell on the man Jared had flown in just this morning.

Courtney's father peered behind Ransom, his face healthy once again and his smile bright. His eyes clear and sober.

"Daddy." She ran over to him and hugged him tight. "I don't understand."

The entire group of men, women and children were grinning. Roscoe held Dylan in his arms and walked over, Velma at his side.

She beamed at both of them. "Welcome to forever, dearie."

Courtney smiled at her son. "Hey, Jelly Bean."

"Ma...ma." He grinned. He turned to Jared. "Da."

Jared took a deep breath. It was now or never.

He knelt down on one knee in front of Courtney and looked up at her. "Courtney Jamison, I know you never imagined yourself living on a ranch in Texas. But if anyone deserves honorary cowgirl status it's you. You're tough, you're determined, you love our son. I'd be honored if you would be my wife, stay with me and let me prove my love for you every day of our lives."

He dug into his pocket and pulled out a small velvet box, and flipped it open. The old-fashioned ring rested against the black, simple, the diamond small. Maybe he should have bought her something glitzy.

"It's beautiful." Tears rolled down her face. "Perfect, and like nothing I would have ever chosen for myself. You see into my heart like no one ever has."

She stood there, silent, staring at him. He squirmed under her gaze.

"Courtney?"

She smiled, her eyes bright with joy. "Of course I'll marry you."

A loud cheer rang out. Jared stood and slipped the ring on her finger. He couldn't help himself, he lowered his lips to hers, slowly, gently, tenderly. Trying with actions to show her what he had so much trouble saying in words.

His heart thudded in his chest and he entwined his fingers with her. "If you don't like the ring—"

"It's mine now. You're mine." She squeezed

his hands. "Haven't you learned by now, I don't need the trimmings. I'm only interested in your heart, Jared King."

His heart overflowing, Jared sent a prayer upwards. Courtney's love had broken the curse of the Last Chance Ranch.

"You have it. Forever. For always."

* * * * *

LET'S TALK
Romance

For exclusive extracts, competitions
and special offers, find us online:

f facebook.com/millsandboon

⊡ @millsandboonuk

🐦 @millsandboon

Or get in touch on 0844 844 1351*

For all the latest titles coming soon,
visit millsandboon.co.uk/nextmonth

*Calls cost 7p per minute plus your phone company's price per
minute access charge

Want even more
ROMANCE?

Join our bookclub today!